For Imogen

Never stop Dreaming

BELLADON : HELL HATH NO FURY

CHAPTER ONE

A thick plume of smoke snaked upwards into the starlit sky, it raced into the night shooting through the broken branches of wounded trees casting a shadow in front of a large white moon. Inside the upturned bonnet of the battered car, small flames began to flicker. A man stepped forwards, an infant girl draped over his hulking shoulder unconscious, her tiny arms dangling limply flapped against his back with soft thuds as he moved. The moonlight illuminated his handsome face showing the dark veins which bustled under his skin, he ground his teeth together in annoyance as he inspected the scene. The driver was dead, that much was clear but the passenger had survived, her chest moving rapidly up and down against the safety belt that had twisted tight across her middle, she fumbled blindly trying to find the clasp to release her from the seat.

"There's no point wasting your energy." He said quietly.

"Baron get me out of here!" The woman begged noticing the vampire for the first time.

"I'm afraid I can't do that Marina." He sighed sounding almost genuinely sorry. "You see, I caused this for a reason." He gestured with his free hand at the mangled carcass of the vehicle. "Even if I were to get you out, you're dying, can't you feel it?" He frowned, his blue eyes cold.

"Why would you do this? We were friends!" Marina whispered tears forming in her eyes, a sharp pain pressed through her back making her groan, the weight of her body slumped heavily against the nylon belt.

"I hate to see you like this, it could have been so different. You could have been a queen!" Baron slammed his fist into the wheel of the car which was spinning crookedly on its axel in the air.

"No Baron, there is no queen of darkness, evil has no master only those who think they can control it. Eventually it will consume you, it always does. I feel sorry for you my friend." Marina grimaced, blood erupting from between her teeth as she began to cough violently.

"I will take care of her." Baron stated hoisting the child more firmly against his shoulder.

"Please I beg you don't take my children, let them live." Marina stretched a hand out of the empty window.

"She won't be killed, if she inherits your power then I will make her a queen when the time is right. Just like you could have been. She will help form a new race." The vampire stated with visible excitement.

"No! If you do this you will leave me no choice, I beg you leave her here to be found. No child should be forced to live with dark magic." Marina shouted her voice cracking with pain.

"No choice? What choice do you have in this any longer?" Baron frowned placing the girl onto the ground and kneeling beside the car. "You were a powerful witch Marina, but you have nothing left to threaten me with."

"Leave her here, I beg you." Marina reached her hand out again hoping to touch the vampire.

"I cannot do that. I told you that I would have to kill you, your betrayal left me no choice. But I will take care of her you have my word on that she will come to no harm." Baron rose to his feet turning his back.

A steady ripple of muffled words reached his ears.

"What are you doing?" He barked spinning around to glare at the woman, her lips moved quickly a trickle of blood spilling from her drooping chin. "Stop!" Baron roared. A moment later silence filled the woods, a thin veil almost invisible in the darkness shimmered between the dying woman and the enraged vampire who was wide eyed and shaking.

"What did you do?" He hissed.

"They will be your undoing, unless you choose another path, they will destroy all that you value and bring death to you in its most absolute form. A curse, but one that can be broken. Let them go Baron, while you are still able." Marina smiled encouragingly, her teeth appearing pink in the light of the moon stained with blood. Her green eyes began to roll back, her head lolled heavy against her chest her outstretched hand fell limp against the ground. The flames under the ruptured sheet of metal suddenly sprang upwards stuttering to life, Baron flinched moving backwards a step avoiding the burst of heat, to his right a something was rapidly moving closer, pounding feet stamping through the long grass, smashing and snapping twigs and bracken. There was no time to question the witch further, he snarled with anger scooped up the child and moved off through the trees out of sight, scrabbling up onto a ledge of rock hiding in shadow he looked down at the remains of the car.

A woman burst through the gap in the trees her hand resting on a sagging branch, the pale yellow innards bleeding sap sticky against her trembling fingers, she seemed to wilt down the embankment crumpling to a halt against the shattered window. She held out a hand and with a faint glow from the palm extinguished the dancing flames. Marina remained still. Baron, having seen enough slid away from his perch and moved deeper into the forest.

"Marina! It's me, Regina." The witch grasped at her sisters cold hand lifting it from the ground into her lap. From the flattened back of the car came a small whimper, barely audible above the hiss of the smoking engine. Regina carefully leaned forwards, pushing her head between folds of metal and the rough upholstery of the seat.

"Regina." A voice whispered against her ear making her jump back into the open air. Marina had one eye cracked open her pupil wide, the green ring no more than a smudge against the bloodshot white.

"Yes sister." Regina scrambled forwards her hands frantically trying to hold up her siblings face. "I will get you out!" She sobbed pulling at the safety belt.

"No, I'm dying 'Gina. You need to get her back, keep them safe. Get my little girl. Ruta..." The words broke into a sickening gurgle, dark crimson sludge slowly dripped from her blueish lips and Marina fell silent, her open eye wide and unseeing.

Regina brought her hand to her mouth stifling a wail of despair as the child began to cry from inside the wreckage, she crawled around the edge of the car looking for a way into the confined space. On the driver's side the door had come completely away leaving a gaping hole behind the lifeless body of the man dangling against the wheel, Regina could see a crop of dark hair and a pair of tiny blood flecked hands scrunched into fists behind the seat. She reached out her hand but the flow of magic wilted under her sorrow, she gestured with the palms upwards but to no avail, the wreckage would not budge.

"Ruta?" She queried gently, smiling through her tears as the child lifted her head carefully.

"I need you to come to me little one." Regina lay flat on her stomach and pressed her fingers forwards clasping the girl's small hand, she felt her pull away but held on none the less.

"It's ok, I am your aunt you are safe with me." Regina pleaded pulling gently, the car creaked with the movement, the metal blackening with the growing fire. Ruta began to cry louder her big eyes looking fearfully towards her mother, she tugged back not wanting to move and Regina lost her grip. To the right a scuffed and singed teddy bear lay, catapulted from the car as it flew through the air, Regina grabbed at it smiling as the heartfelt crying subsided from the shadows.

"Mr Bear says he needs you to come and give him a hug, he fell an awfully long way and says only you can make him better." She held the bear carefully using her fingers to push its blackened paw outwards. Tentative shuffling sounds reached her ears and she beamed with relief as a little face squeezed its way through the gap followed by a body, arms and finally two legs and feet minus a shoe. Ruta was bloodstained and muddied, a red welt over one eye and a cut bottom lip where her teeth had bitten into it, she reached for the bear and pulled him close pieces of glass shining in the skin of her narrow arm. Regina grabbed at her with relief, holding her tightly to her chest one hand pressed against the back of her head she rose to her feet and with her heart breaking began to walk away as the fire from the engine reignited.

"Mamma!" The child lifted her head to gaze over Regina's shoulder.

"We have to leave mamma behind now, she has gone from this world." Regina's legs almost crumpled as Ruta threw herself forwards arms outstretched, the bear clutched firmly in her fist as she wailed.

"I want my mamma!" She screamed her chest heaving as she wriggled to get free. Regina fell forwards, the jolt silencing Ruta's screams, she gripped the tiny shoulders tightly, a stream of words rolling from her lips angrily, the child seemed dazed.

"She is dead! Don't you understand she is gone! You can scream if you wish but it will not bring her back." Tears streamed from the lavender eyes of the witch. "She is gone!" She sobbed, her arms falling loose at her sides. She raised her trembling hands and clasped them over her face unable to bear the pain radiating through her body. Minutes passed and gradually Regina regained her senses, the racking sobs subsided and she realised for the first time that a narrow pair of arms were looped tightly around her neck, she opened her reddened eyes and felt Ruta's warm breath against her cheek, the dark hair stuck to the trail of tears which ran along her skin, she was calmer now, the memory spell must have worked taking the edge off the pain she had seen.

Regina rose to her feet soundlessly, clutching the girl tight to her chest and once again began to walk.

CHAPTER TWO

It was beginning to get light when I opened my eyes, sweat dotted my face and stuck my hair slick against the back of my neck making me shiver in the cold. My blankets felt damp too, I kicked them off bracing against the frost as I jumped up and grabbed two more from the fresh pile stacked in the bottom of my wardrobe. It had become a regular occurrence to be woken by nightmares. Tonight's had been particularly hard, any memory of Barry always was, he had reached up to me from the black and white floor begging me to save him, his chest scarred with a hole where his heart had been. I shuddered at the image and wrapped the thick woven material tightly around my body. Three months had passed since the funerals took place, three long months since the witches had returned to the cavern in the mountainside. My sister Mia and I had decided to stay at the castle for a while, I wanted to complete my training as a medical assistant (much to my aunts disgust, she wanted me to start harnessing any magical ability I may have immediately) and Mia wanted to just be a kid for a while, she wanted to take lessons, to make friends, play sports, all the boring stuff that she had never experienced. I took a swig from a glass of water and threw a log onto the burning embers in my tiny fireplace, staring at the minute red sparks that flew up knowing it wouldn't be enough to actually get the piece of wood burning. Across the room a small basket of straw and a box of matches lay discarded, I could get up and reignite the fire it would take only a few minutes. My breath puffed out clouds from under the safety of the blankets, reminding me how cold it was out in the open. Releasing a hand from the covers, I stretched my fingertips forwards almost touching the metal grate that held the slightly smouldering log. I strained forwards, my mind urging a spark to jump from my semi numb fingertips. As usual nothing happened! Sighing I dived out of bed, grabbed the matches and a fistful of straw and threw it into the fire place striking a match against the floor, I hovered, hopping from foot to foot making sure the little stick caused a flame amongst the golden tubes.

"Ruta are you awake!" Mia dashed through the door her eyes darting from the empty bed to where I stood shivering. "Oh good your awake!" She smiled and jumped onto my mattress.

"Well it's a good thing I am or you would be in serious trouble." I told her grumpily.

She held out the blankets wrapping them over her shoulders and inviting me to join her.

"I just finished reading the most wonderful story I had to come and tell you about it." She gushed pressing a leather bound book into my hands. I turned the cover over and examined it in the growing light.

"The jungle book? You risked waking me up at…" I glanced at the clock on my shelf "at five thirty in the morning to tell me about the jungle book?" I stared at her.

"Have you read it? Its amazing Ruta!" She grinned.

"Oh my God we need to get you some different reading material." I groaned sliding down the bed and resting my head against the pillow.

"I like these stories. They have happy endings." Mia muttered quietly.

"I know you do." I yawned loudly.

"Do you think Greta will come and visit soon?" Mia asked. Greta the young witch who lived in the coven with our Aunt had not taken very well to us not returning to the cavern with the witches, especially since Mia had become such a close friend of hers.

"I don't know Mia. She'll get over it, it's not as if you're never going to see her again. We're going back there next month anyway, she will have to speak to you once we're there." I assured her.

"She didn't even come for our birthday though. She must be so mad." Mia sighed tucking a strand of her bobbed black hair squarely behind her ear.

"She needs to grow up and stop being such a brat." I stated firmly.

In the fireplace the log began to crackle and flames dithered around its edges throwing strange shadows against the walls.

"Do you still have the dreams?" Mia whispered as she lay down beside me.

"Every night." I told her.

"Me too." She answered burrowing her head against my shoulder.

"I can't believe they are dead. It just seemed to be over so quickly, I almost feel as if it's a trick, as if it's just a pause. The calm before the storm so to speak." I spoke to myself more than to my sister.

"Don't say that Ruta. I don't think I could bear any more darkness, not now, not after knowing what the world can be like." Mia's voice wavered and I wrapped my arm tightly around her.

"No you're right, I'm just being silly worrying for no reason. We are safe now, everything is fine." The words left a bitter taste in my mouth, a wave of nausea passed over me making me want to sit up and vomit, the same leaden cold feeling I had every day washed across my chest compressing the air in my lungs like an iron belt. If everything was fine, why did I have this constant feeling of dread?

"You're worried, I can tell." Mia said gently.

"I just have a suspicious nature." I tried to force a laugh. Mia stayed silent but I could feel her body tense, her eyes blinking back tears as her mind raced through possibilities.

"Come on." I sat up tugging her with me, skipping out of bed and reaching for some thick black woollen trousers.

"Where are we going?" Mia's green eyes were wide.

"You are going to your room to get dressed, then we are going to meet at the bottom of the stairs and arm you with my favourite books from the library. You think the jungle book is good, wait until you become acquainted with Harry." I grinned as I pulled on a heavy sweater, Mia frowned slightly pausing as she reached for the latch of my door.

"Who's Harry? Does he work in there?" She queried.

I gawped at her not knowing whether to laugh or just feel sad for the years that she had missed, I went with the latter and tears began to prickle at my eyes, the silliest things could remind you of the hardest.

"You'll see. Get dressed." It was the best I could manage.

CHAPTER THREE

Tom sniffed warily at the edge of his lair, his crushed ribs had healed almost completely leaving only slight pain in the surrounding muscle, but resting for so long had made him thin, his coat stood on end, dull and matted in places. He lifted his snout and pushed a stray conifer branch aside letting his muzzle edge into the crisp morning air. For weeks he had been tracking the remaining smell of Vincent, a vampire that was meant to be dead, from the edge of the hidden cave up towards a rock face in the hills. The scent was barely noticeable, every inch of the trail took days to weed out amongst the melting snow and animal tracks and even when he had made progress, it appeared to lead to a dead end. Vincent was alive, Tom had no doubt about that, but where he had vanished to was a mystery that even his sharp senses couldn't unravel. The werewolf moved forwards, quickly slipping down the slope and out of view into the tightly packed web of trees, he loped between the trunks and patches of rock his sharp ears spinning like radar's alert for any sound. He had given himself two more days to try to find Vincent, if he had no luck after that he would go to the cavern of the witches and inform Regina of what he knew, two days was all he could manage, the wild animals had vanished from the area and his injuries had made it impossible to venture too far. He sniffed once or twice, the iron scent all but gone, raising his yellow eyes into the glare of the winter sun he focused on the wall of rock high up a mile or so away. Vincent had come this way, the scent led directly to the towering outcrop, Tom lay flat under the branches of a nearby tree, placing his nose against his front paws and settled down to keep watch once more.

Deep inside the hidden cave Vincent lay staring at the ceiling from his camp bed, the bones of mice and rabbits littered the far corner piled unceremoniously atop one another. His hand rested against his stomach, moving in time with each slow breath. Above him the faded picture of a popstar smiled jovially back, her eyes gleaming as she held a microphone before her lips.

"I wonder if she's a millionaire by now." Vincent mused with a smile.

"I have no idea." Marina answered quietly, her lips were bruised and split.

"Oh come now! Are you still sulking? I wouldn't have had to hit you that hard if you had been quiet like I told you." Vincent sat up and tugged the khaki sweater he was wearing down at the back.

"He will eventually find this place you know, he's already close by. If I was strong enough my mind would reach him." Marina hissed.

Vincent balled his fist tightly and boomed it against the wall making the woman flinch further into the shadows. He sighed trying to regain his composure.

"He has been out there for weeks! He isn't going to find you, he hasn't got much left in him anyway he's as thin as a rake. He will have to move on to somewhere else, no doubt he will head to the witches, predictable as always." Vincent stroked his small pointed beard a smirk tugging at the corners of his lips. "My brother was a fool to trust him in the first place, he's nothing but an unwanted mutt."

"He knows the meaning of loyalty." Marina whispered.

"Loyalty? Yes that's a good characteristic for a dog." Vincent laughed rising to his feet and tugging open the roughly made door he walked away up the sloping corridor which had been dug into the earth, ducking his head in the darkness to avoid the familiar tips of protruding rocks. He edged carefully through the inky black sidestepping a drop and hopping up to a ledge where a set of tangled tree roots crawled through the wall and down into the abyss. Between the web small pinpricks of light shot through into the dark, beads of dust scattering and dancing in the minute spotlights. Vincent pressed his eye to one of the larger holes and holding his breath scanned the forest and mountain slope below looking for the werewolf, his fingers gripped into the dirt holding him steady against the wall. As much as he had played down any worry in front of Marina the truth was Vincent was all too aware that the wolf was merely a step away from finding the entrance to his hiding place. It wasn't so much the thought of a fight that bothered the vampire it was more the thought of Tom fleeing to Regina and bringing back reinforcements. His plan would only work if nobody knew for sure he had survived. He held his gaze out into the open for a few minutes longer, there was no movement, not even a rabbit. Vincent moved away silently.

If he had been a little more patient he may have noticed the slight waver in a low conifer branch, the drop of a heavy pile of melting snow, the crack of a branch as a skinny wolf shot through the trees. Tom ran through the burning pain in his lungs, he pushed his trembling legs faster than he thought he could, the flash of the cold ice blue eye had been enough to tell the werewolf that Vincent was somewhere behind the upturned tree that dangled over the twisted rocks. With enough power that tree could be pulled out, with magic it could even be done silently. He grinned baring his yellowed fangs, tongue lolling from his mouth and pounded steadily on, it wasn't far to the cavern he would reach Regina before nightfall.

"So you finally made it here then." Greta said sullenly. She was huddled cross legged next to the smouldering logs of the fire pit her narrow face resting on her hands as she watched a witch adding spices to the giant cauldron that simmered over the flames. I looked at Mia as I pulled down the bags that were dangling from the horse's saddle, we had only just arrived after hours of trekking in the cold up and over the rocky slopes and a bratty kid was the last thing I needed.

"Hey Greta give her a break." I turned around sharply depositing my ruck sack heavily on the ground and placing my hands on my hips.

"It's ok Ruta." Mia jumped in quickly as Greta rose to her feet opening her mouth to reply. "I'm sorry I didn't come back with you all, but we're here now." My sister the peace maker, she smiled sheepishly. "I just wanted to see what life was like at Belladon, we were always going to be coming back here though you're our family."

Greta poked her bare toe into the earth and shrugged her shoulders a little.

"I just missed you." She murmured.

"I missed you too." Mia sprang forward hugging the girl tightly and the pair quickly fell to laughing.

"Great, now that we've got that out of the way maybe we can eat?" I looked hopefully at the witch who was stirring the mixture in the pot.

"Oh it's not quite ready yet." A voice I knew well materialised behind me and I turned, smiling broadly.

"Regina!" I held my arms out as my Aunt slammed into my chest gripping me with force.

"Hello girls." She said stretching across to place a hand gently atop the crown of Mia's head.

"We made it." I laughed following my Aunt as she moved around the fire pit and took a seat on one of the upturned logs.

"Yes you did." She returned my smile, her lavender eyes scanning me over, flicking past my shoulder to look at Mia who was chattering busily to Greta. "How is she?" She asked quietly.

"She's doing ok." I nodded slowly, even though we were twins my sister somehow seemed younger than me, her life held captive by Baron had kept her stuck in a childlike mentality. "I think it did her good to be at the castle for a while, there's so many people to mix with. She had no shortage of friends." We had become the talking point of the entire castle and of course everyone wanted to be Mia's best friend, just like any other place where a new girl comes in. I however had been avoided like the plague, people connected all the trouble to me after all I was the one who had been the focal point of the attack in the dining hall, it was my best friend who had his heart ripped out.

"What about you?" Regina placed a hand on to the denim covering my knee.

"Oh I'm fine." I told her shaking off the unwanted memories. My Aunt stared at me hard but didn't push it any further.

"Can Mia share my room?" Greta interrupted her face shining eagerly.

"Yes that's fine." Regina told her with a smile.

"Come on!" Greta giggled pulling Mia away into a corridor on the far side of the room.

"You look uneasy." Regina commented in little more than a whisper.

"I feel it." I admitted. "Something doesn't feel right." I ran a hand through a strand of untucked hair pushing it back into place.

"How do you mean?" She shuffled closer.

"I don't know. It just feels like I'm waiting for something to happen." I moaned. I expected my Aunt to reassure me but she said nothing and just sat staring into the red embers with her mouth pulled tight into a hard line. "This is the part where you're supposed to tell me I'm being silly and that everything is fine." I added.

"I could tell you that" Regina sighed and fixed her eyes upon mine. "But I fear I would be telling you a lie. I feel the same way and I have learnt it's unwise to mistrust your instincts."

"What do you know?" I asked heavily.

"I don't know anything for sure." Regina sighed. "But I believe that we have missed something, it feels wrong, it feels, as you say, like we are merely waiting, but for what I have no clue." We resumed our silence, around us the cavern was bustling with life, people laughed, animals called to one and other, plates where being scrubbed and dried and laid out on the long trestle table ready for dinner, life was continuing on oblivious to the turmoil and fear that was resting against my heart.

"How are you anyway?" I asked turning in my seat.

"Oh I am fine." Regina ran a hand through her loose dark hair, a movement I knew mirrored my own habit.

"Vincent can't have been all bad." I said even though it grated against every nerve.

"No. At least I don't think so." She shook her head and her eyes flashed with the flickering of the fire. "I'm not sure of anything anymore." She muttered.

"You really loved him." It was a statement not a question but my aunt answered anyway.

"Yes. With every inch of my heart." She looked back up into my face with defiance, obviously she had come under fire a few times for it after all he and his brother had done. I held my hands in the air.

"I'm not judging." I told her.

"Sorry." She sighed "Some are not so open minded." She glanced over her shoulder at a cluster of older women who were watching us closely.

"Regina! Regina!" Anita came trundling red faced towards us.

"What is it?" Regina was on her feet in a flash.

"Somebody is coming!" the witch panted heavily pointing up towards the ceiling. Regina closed her eyes, her brow furrowing as she concentrated, the cavern fell still.

"It's ok!" She laughed after what seemed like an eternity of silence. "Anita open the entrance." Anita cocked her head and raised a chubby hand to her chest.

"Regina are you sure?" She stuttered.

"Yes, I'm more than sure! Open it up." My Aunt cried loudly a grin spreading from ear to ear.

Anita moved across the open space and placed her fingertip gingerly onto a sharp point of rock pressing down until a single bead of claret appeared, she placed the liquid against a smooth stone and muttered a few words and with a crack the hidden lift began to descend. The rope pulleys squeaked noisily drawing the attention of every witch, even Mia and Greta had reappeared and were staring upwards hands clutched tightly together.

Slowly four furry feet came into view, shaking and splayed to balance out the weight of the skeletal body above.

"Tom!" Mia screamed running forwards as the slab of rock swung to a halt. The wolf all but collapsed in her arms.

"Sisters! Food, blankets now!" Regina commanded moving towards Tom who was panting heavily his legs twitching back and forth. A flurry of movement enveloped the wolf who with a half growl half groan reverted to his human form. Every bone in his body was protruding, his ribs parted with deep gaps as he drew in shallow breaths.

"Tom." Regina was at his side piling the blankets around him, he flopped his head into the folds his eyes unfocused into the crowd of witches.

"I found him." He muttered, his eyes rolling as he searched for Regina's face.

"Take him to the healer." Regina stood back as four women swept in and carefully using the blankets as a hammock carried him out of sight.

"What did he mean?" I asked as my aunt paced back and forth.

"I don't know Ruta." She held a hand up at me distractedly as she walked.

"I could see it." Greta said carefully, her face pale as everyone turned to look.

"Speak then!" Regina barked, aware of the young girl's mind reading talents.

"He found Vincent." A gasp rustled through the gathering crowd.

"Impossible you must have seen the past, he's dead!" Regina frowned.

"No he isn't." Greta shook her head. "He traced him, clever vampire tricked us all. He's hidden behind a wall of rock, that's why it took him so long, Tom, he couldn't find the entrance but then he saw him, he saw his eye behind the tree roots." She was talking quickly panic in her voice. Greta let out a sharp squeal and looked up directly at me before her eyes clouded over, milky white and she slumped to the ground. Mia screamed.

"Don't touch her!" Regina dashed forwards pulling my twin sister back roughly, a circle of space spread out around the girl who was now rolling back and forth on the floor.

"What is happening to her?" Mia cried.

"Something very rare, she's gone inside Tom's mind and from that she has looped into the memories of Vincent himself, eye to eye contact means she can see what he saw." Regina was leaning forwards her chest heaving.

"How is that even possible?" I gawped.

"It is extremely rare. If she were to look into your eyes and search out a particular person who you had come into contact with or someone who was very strong or powerful that you had encountered, with time and practice she would be able to view their memories also." Greta arched upwards off the ground her shoulders and heels the only thing in contact with the surface, then with a heavy thud she collapsed and her eyes returned to normal.

"Greta what did you see?" Regina was kneeling at her side as she panted for breath.

"It can't be real." Greta began to cry shaking her head from side to side.

"Greta tell me what you saw!" Regina placed her hands on either side of the girls face.

"I saw a woman, imprisoned in a hole in a mountain, bruised and tormented, weakened held captive for a very long time." Greta wept. "I could feel her magic but she can't make it work, every day staring at darkness."

"What did she look like?" Regina asked.

"She looked like her." Greta raised a shaking hand to point at me. "But older." A wave of ice cold fear washed across my body and I stumbled back a step.

"They thought she was dead, she cried for her children." Greta continued in a warbling voice. "He pulled her out of the car, he got her out after his brother left, he never knew she had survived. Baron had a plan but he had his own all along." Regina had fallen back off her haunches and was staring wide eyed at the girl in front of her.

"It can't be can it?" I struggled with the words, Mia was gazing back and forth unsure where to look for an answer.

"I don't think Greta is wrong." Regina whispered. "Her talent is too raw to be manipulated, Tom was so desperate to tell us his mind was screaming out to be heard and she heard it and more." Silence enveloped us.

"I'm sorry I couldn't see anymore it just went black." Greta whimpered.

"No child. You have done an incredible thing." Regina stretched out a hand and patted the bare leg before her. "Mia take Greta to go and eat, she needs food."

"I don't understand, who is the woman?" Mia asked as she pulled her friend to her feet. I met my aunt's eye before answering and she gave a curt nod.

"It's our Mother Mia, Vincent has our mother."

CHAPTER FOUR

Greta had given us the information, but not the whereabouts to be able to do anything about it. Tom still lay unconscious a full day after his arrival and even though she had tried as hard as possible Greta could not reach back into his mind.

"We need to get him back to Belladon." I said for the tenth time that hour.

"Yes I agree." Mia said in what was meant to be a firm voice as her cheeks flushed with embarrassment.

"They have everything there that he needs to be able to bring him round again and get him back in good health." I added.

"It is too dangerous to travel with Vincent still out there." Regina repeated.

"We can fight!" Greta bared her teeth, her ragged dress and bare dirty feet gave her a feral look that made me believe she would happily attack an enemy of Vincent's size and strength and even quite possibly win. Nobody commented but everyone smiled.

"There are maps in the castle that show every inch of these mountains, surely if we worked on a radius we would find these cliffs somewhere? With maps on the internet too we could even see if there was an upturned tree through the side of one." I pleaded, a few witches looked at me with confusion.

"Maps?" Anita frowned at me.

"It's hard to explain." I said quickly before continuing. "Look I can't sit here another day. Sixteen years he's had her prisoner, I don't even want to think about what she's gone through. We didn't know she was out there then but we do now." I rose to my feet.

"She's right." Anita nodded withering slightly as Regina fixed her with feline slanted pupils.

"We don't have a choice, we have to go. If Tom dies what then?" I asked.

"He won't die." Mia muttered.

"He might Mia, I'm sorry but it's the truth." Greta wrapped an arm around her protectively and glared in my direction. "If the worst happens we still won't know where to go or what to do until we go to the castle and look at those maps."

Regina stared at me, her hands wringing around each other, she bit her bottom lip.

"Ok." A sigh seemed to rattle through the onlookers, whether it was relief or dread I couldn't tell. "We will leave for the castle tonight." Her voice rose up "Everyone who wishes to come is more than welcome, however no children, sick or wounded this isn't going to be an easy trip and besides, we need people here to tend the animals and look after the homestead."

I began to move away when my Aunt caught me by the arm. "You come with me." She pulled me to one side quickly turning into the narrow corridor that led to her private quarters.

I trailed my hand over the rough wall of hardened earth, my finger tip bumping over the edges of stones, we stepped into Regina's room I gazed around as she quietly shut the door.

"I've never been in here." I mumbled.

"You and Mia are going to be an open moving target." Regina hissed.

"Whatever is going on he must have a plan, he can't be that far away, he would have had to be close to Baron's lair and to the cavern otherwise he would have had to explain the absences of time when he went to tend to Marina. Plus I know him, he wouldn't want her too far away." She paused her eyes widening.

"What?" I questioned.

"He wouldn't want her out of his sight!" Regina flung open the door and sprinted out of sight, I hurried after her.

"Wait!" I shouted.

"Ruta what's happening?" Sarro was at my side tall and stern she followed my eyes to a narrow path in the wall that curled upwards, Regina was flying across the ground her feet barely seeming to touch down.

"Where is she going?" I panted catching my breath as we set off after her.

"The lookout." Sarro moved ahead of me, the old injury in her leg gave her a lolloping, rolling gait but still she covered the ground almost effortlessly. I pounded up the circling slope clutching my side to fight off the cramp that was gnawing at my stomach, lowering my head and powering forwards so that I had to skid to a stop as I broke out into the air. Sarro placed a hand on my shoulder halting me as I walked towards the ledge, the evening had begun to draw in pulling across its darkened blanket, I felt a little dizzy looking across the forest canopy we were so high up even the tallest treetops lay below us.

Regina sat on her haunches, her back to us.

"All this time." She sounded as though she were crying. Sarro closed her eyes and nodded, I had forgotten she also could read minds.

"You couldn't have known." Sarro spoke in a low but firm voice.

"I should have!" Regina shouted, she leapt to her feet and for one horrifying moment teetered on the very edge of the rock face before turning nimbly and moving towards us.

"None of us knew, I can see into minds and still I never knew." Sarro reached out her hand but Regina was pacing from side to side her eyes filled with tears.

"We used to come up here every morning and every evening, Vincent said it was our place." The tears spilled from her eyes but she wiped at them angrily. "The first kiss we ever had, it was here." She gave a short laugh.

"I don't understand." I told her.

"He wouldn't want her out of sight." Regina said pointedly.

"Yeah I know you said that but..." I didn't get a chance to finish what I was saying, my aunt grabbed me by the back of the neck shoving me forwards as she pressed her face next to mine.

"Straight ahead Ruta what do you see?" Her voice wavered. I strained my eyes into the greying sky, scanning the horizon, it took a moment before I saw it, a towering arching wall of rock and compacted earth, almost hemming in the right side of the forest, it looked smooth like clay apart from one dark crack where a squiggle of bending lines marred its surface.

"That looks very much like an upturned tree to me." Regina whispered releasing me from her grip.

"He literally had her in his sight." Sarro shook her head, her long dark hair braided into a plait swung across her shoulders like a pendulum, her fingers twitched at a curved black dagger belted at her waist. "All this time."

Regina flopped onto the floor again, her bare legs pale against the dirt, I had never seen her look so defeated, softly I sat beside her.

"We will find her." I placed my hand on the velvet of her dress.

"This was where we talked about all of our plans, our hopes and dreams." She gazed out, her eyes unfocused as she replayed memories in her mind.

"He did love you Regina. I'm sure of it." I leant in and breathed a sigh of relief as she lifted her arm to wrap around me, I placed my head under her chin.

"I can't believe your mother is still alive Ruta. How will she ever forgive me for not searching for her? For letting you and Mia almost die? For not saving Mia from all of those years trapped underground with vampires?" Regina sagged against me.

"None of that is your fault and she'll know that." I hugged her tiny frame tighter. "I would think she will be happy that you fought for us and that we fought for her, she probably thinks her daughters are dead, maybe he even told her that! Imagine how she's going to feel when she sees us."

"She's right." Sarro sat down beside us. "Marina will be overjoyed that her girls are safe and well."

"I hope you are both right. Marina was one of the strongest witches I have ever known, the thought of her anger, of the darkness she has had to endure, if it has blackened her heart, she would be uncontrollable." Regina sniffed back a tear but her warning filled me with dread. How could anyone remain in control of themselves after being confined for sixteen years, with the sorrow and grief of losing two infant daughters and their father, not knowing if they are alive or dead or imprisoned by a monster like Baron? If we managed to find her and free her, what kind of woman would we be releasing?

CHAPTER FIVE

I ducked my head under the low hanging branch of a giant conifer crouching flat against Matisse's wide neck, the horse strode ahead planting his feet solidly one after the other. Mia and Greta walked beside me chattering happily, each holding a woven rope attached to the halter of a skittering, long legged yearling. The youngster snorted and hopped over the exposed tree roots as though they were snakes his eyes bulging, ears pricked so much so that they were almost meeting in the middle. I knew how he felt. I scanned the trees for the hundredth time imaging Vincent lurking behind one of them, watching us waiting to make his move. The truth was that it would be more than easy for him to attack us on this narrow path, he wouldn't even need any help from any of the vampires who may have survived. After all it was only really Mia and I that he would probably want. Regina looked over her shoulder at me her brow creased into a frown, gently she leant forwards and whispered into the cocked ear of her horse and the grey mare stepped nimbly back to fall in alongside me.

"You have a black cloud around you." She stated.

"I just want to get to the castle quickly." I tried to shake off the fear knotting in my stomach.

"We won't let anything happen to you Ruta." Regina leant over and placed a hand on my shoulder.

"It's not too far now anyway is it?" I smiled.

"No, about an hour or so." Regina replaced her hand on the narrow neck of the mare and stroked a piece of shining mane. "We could move quicker, but with Tom being carried it just is not possible." We both looked over to our right where four witches held the long poles carrying the blanket sling with the werewolf atop it.

"He looks so young." I whispered.

"He is barely ten years older than you. He's had a hard life though and he bears the scars to prove it." Regina flicked her eyes to my face. "As do you." She added.

"Are you trying to say I look old!?" I gasped but my aunt merely laughed and nudged her horse away.

The gravelled moat crunching below the procession of feet was a welcome sound. I watched Mia dart ahead to meet her friends who were eagerly awaiting on the castle steps, embracing them with squeals of delight, Greta wore a sour expression as she looked on.

"Hey, you will always be her best friend." I told her, she shrugged nonchalantly but her face relaxed a little.

"Miss Ottoman." Mr Bard wheeled himself towards us a line of burly young men following closely behind, hunter's no doubt following their tutor.

"Which one?" Regina asked with amusement.

"The younger one." Bard turned to face me. "Take the horses to the stables please." He wasn't addressing anyone in particular but the boys moved forwards and took the reins. Matisse snorted and bared his teeth at the contact.

"These animals aren't like normal beasts." Regina slid out of the saddle and onto the floor silently. "Do not make the mistake of manhandling them. Just ask them to follow you and they will." The students nodded quickly and a muttering of come this way please echoed across the grounds. I grinned and jumped down as Matisse moved away.

"You could have waited for me to get off!" I called after him, he nickered in reply. "I swear he laughs at me!" I grumbled.

"Mr Belladon is waiting for you in the dining room." Mr Bard instructed. "The rest of you may follow me, obviously we knew of your impending arrival and have cleared one of our billets to accommodate your stay." He began to pull away to the left.

"Mr Bard our friend is badly injured and needs medical attention, immediately." I said quickly. The witches moved forwards bringing Tom into sight.

"I thought that werewolf was dead?" Bard ground his teeth. "I'm sure he has a grave not so far away."

"Well he isn't." Mia said bravely. "He needs help."

"Take him to Dr Vause." Bard barked as he pushed on the wheels of his chair. Two more muscular boys moved forward and carefully took the handles of the stretcher jogging towards the medical centre. "At least if he dies there's already a hole."

"He will be fine now Mia." Anita rubbed her shoulders comfortingly ignoring Bard's snarl. "Come on, let's get settled in." She guided the girls towards the forest.

"Regina, you're coming with me right?" I asked nervously pulling on her arm.

"Of course." She said sternly, linking her hand with mine as we climbed the steps.

"Welcome, welcome, welcome!" Henry Belladon hobbled forwards resting heavily on his cane.

"Hello sir." I said respectfully.

"Henry." Regina nodded and moved towards the fireplace which was crackling with logs.

"How are you Ruta?" He took my hand and looked at me hard.

"I'm ok." I smiled.

"So what brings you to our gates in such numbers, surely not just a visit however welcome that may always be? You have an injured wolf with you as well so I hear?" He gestured to the seats near the hearth and I took one gratefully.

"Vincent Hill is alive." Regina stated. The crystal top of the decanter in Henry's hand clattered to the floor rolling out of sight.

"Impossible!" He spluttered.

"It's true." I told him. He stayed silent for a few minutes gawping between me and my aunt, then with shaking hands poured out a rather large measure of whiskey.

"Well if you say it, I don't doubt your knowledge." He leant over the back of the chair towards us and I quickly relieved him of the two square glasses he held out. He moved slowly around the room and flopped into an armchair, his gaunt features illuminated by the fire.

"Is he dangerous?" He asked looking at Regina.

"He's a vampire and a liar, he couldn't be anything but." Regina downed her drink in one.

"There's more." She handed her glass to me and nodded towards the whiskey. I stood and poured another hefty measure.

"Go on." Henry sipped at his own drink.

"Marina is alive." Regina sank the new drink in one but this time sat her glass down on the nearby table.

"Now that *is* impossible!" Henry stuttered.

"I assure you, it isn't." Regina sat on the floor before the flickering flames crossing her legs and fixing him with a stare. The old man looked at me for help, but all I could do was nod. Regina told him everything, how Greta had seen into Tom's mind, how Vincent had my mother imprisoned. In the end there was only a disbelieving silence.

"This can't be happening." Henry mumbled. "It doesn't bare thinking about, all those years." He shook his head tears dotting his eyes. "Your mother would be..." He stifled a sob.

"My mother would bring down a wrath upon Vincent like nothing this world has ever seen." Regina hissed, her lilac eyes seemed to glow with anger. "And I will do the same."

A tap at the huge mahogany doors made us all turn, the handle flexed and the wood creaked open.

"Sorry to interrupt, but I just heard you were here." Hannah appeared, I smiled and began to say hello but the only person she seemed aware of was my aunt. Regina hopped to her feet and crossed the room embracing her with both arms.

"It's good to see you." I heard her mutter. Henry looked at me with a crooked smile and tilt of his head that made us both stifle a laugh. Aware that the embrace had gone on slightly longer than usual Regina pulled back and patted herself down before coming towards us.

"Are you blushing?" I whispered as she took a seat beside me.

"Shut up!" She growled through clenched white teeth.

"Miss Shaw it is very good to see you again." Henry held out a hand for her to shake, which she did before sitting down.

"Hi Ruta." She smiled and pushed a strand of her blonde hair from her eyes back behind her ear. "So what's happening? Anything interesting going on?" She asked. Regina and I looked at each other, the moment of joviality quickly gone.

"You may want to pour yourself a drink." Henry said heavily.

CHAPTER SIX

"So that's the plan?" I asked looking around the table at the assembled faces of witches and hunters. Mr Bard had a huge yellowing map splayed in front of him.

"Yes." He nodded.

"We just go straight up to this solid rock face, that has God knows what or who inside and we attack it?" I looked at my aunt who was also looking less than happy.

"Yes." Bard growled.

"The witches can lift the tree clear?" Henry was chewing his lip nervously.

"Yes, but it won't go unnoticed, the noise and vibration of something that big pulling out of the earth will be immense. Plus we need to make sure that it only moves a few feet so that we can still use the trunk as a ramp to gain entrance." Sarro spoke, she too didn't look convinced.

"This is a bad plan." I said crossing my arms.

"What are you thinking Ruta?" Henry asked holding up a hand to silence the protest of the hunting tutor who was becoming redder in the face, his goatee beard bristling.

"Well I don't know exactly, but I think if we go charging in, by the time we actually move the tree there could be an army of Vampires waiting for us on the other side, or he could kill my mother and then get away through a secret tunnel and we won't have gained anything. Right now as far as we know, Vincent has no idea we even know where he is. If we can get in there without being noticed we may have a chance to either find out what we are facing." I took a breath.

"Or kill him before he knows what's coming." Regina added.

"That's simple enough to say but not do." Bard gave a harsh laugh.

"Not if only a small group went in." Hannah countered quietly. "If you have enough power to move an entire tree, surely you could make a hole in the earth where it is already broken through, crumble it away or something? It would be much quieter and would give enough space for a few of us to get in and see what we are dealing with. If one of the telepaths comes with us we can even send messages back to an attack force waiting out of sight if need be." The room fell silent.

"I think that's a good idea." I nodded.

"As do I." Regina agreed.

"Yes I think it is a much safer option." Henry looked around the table.

"No!" Bard bellowed making everyone jump. "They need to be wiped out! Move the tree and throw all of our force into there, grenades, guns, missile launchers, blow the whole place up! Set it into flames and dust! Send in my hunters, not some would be heroes. My team is already on the ground scouting out any hidden exits, we can bury them alive." Small white bits of spittle where flying from his mouth, his eyes bulging and cheeks red.

"My sister is in there." Regina said quietly.

"She won't even be worth saving after all this time with filthy vampires! Do you really think she will be the same person? She could be staying there out of choice! Who knows, it may run in the family, the affection for this vampire, she could be in love with him as well!" Bard was shouting. In an instant Regina was on her feet and across the table knocking glasses of water all over the smooth wooden surface, she held the spluttering man by his throat his eyes bulging with surprise.

"I understand your anger, you lost your legs, your friends, your loved ones." Regina said quietly. "But if you speak like that again, you will lose even more of your body parts, do you understand?"

"Regina, let him go." Hannah had stepped forwards and placed her hand over Regina's which was clasped tightly around Bard's throat. The hunters behind him were shifting from foot to foot restlessly, glaring at the witches who had risen to their feet. Regina released her grip and jumped down with barely a thud before leaving the room.

"She touches me again and I'll kill her myself." Bard coughed a few times, shrugging off the hands of his concerned students angrily. "I'm fine!" He snapped. "This is the type of person you want to send to deal with vampires?" He was glaring at Henry who was leaning heavily on his crutch.

"I don't know what you are surprised by Mr Bard." He hopped a few steps and slid into his favourite armchair by the fire. "You just insulted a woman who has lost more than she can bear to think of, you reminded her of every failing she thinks she has and insulted a sister she has thought was dead for over a decade. Did you think she would smile and thank you for your critique?" I supressed a grin, however incompetent Henry Belladon was at physical combat, he could certain slay with words. Mr Bard ground his teeth, his lips drawn back in a snarl.

"I want my best team going in first. If these witches want to follow afterwards, that's up to them." He said quietly.

"Deal." Henry smiled. "I'm glad we fixed this little dilemma, now I'm sure you all need to get prepared?"

"Let's go." Bard snapped his fingers and was pushed briskly from the room. I took a seat next to Henry who was rubbing at his temples.

"Are you ok?" I asked, he seemed so much older now, thin and crumpled at the waist, his iron grey suit slightly frayed at the edge and white hair combed back.

"Yes. I just don't know what is going to happen Ruta. If Anise were here, well, she would know exactly what to do and everyone would be put to task in exactly the right way." He smiled.

"I would have loved to know her better." I swallowed down a wave of sadness.

"Ah, she would have loved you and your sister. You wouldn't have had a moment's peace though." He laughed. "She would have had you practicing magic and doing all kinds of crazy things to try and bring out whatever is hidden inside you." I wilted, I had completely forgotten that by now I really should have been showing some kind of ability, that's if there was anything there at all. Henry sensed the sag in my mood and patted my knee kindly.

"Don't you worry, it will appear as soon as you are ready I have no doubt about it." We fell into a comfortable silence, listening to the padding feet in the corridor outside as everyone gathered the things they would need.

"You know, I hate to say it Ruta but I am also worried about how Marina may have been affected." Henry admitted.

"I'm sure if she's as everyone has always said, kind and generous and clever, then, I'm sure those things will have carried her through. Look at Mia, she never turned to darkness and she was a kid growing up in a hole in the ground surrounded with nothing but creatures who wanted to kill her or use her blood! It must be something in our genes, some kind of stubbornness." I picked at a seam on my jeans trying to control the thundering of my heart.

"I'm sure you're right." Henry tried to smile.

The doors swung open and Hannah appeared red faced and out of breath she signalled me to follow her with her arm.

"Tom's awake."

CHAPTER SEVEN

Seeing Tom propped up on the green pillows of the medical wing felt strange, like seeing something in a place it just shouldn't be. His face was still grey, sunken in at the cheeks but he was smiling his lazy smile and drinking soup from a bowl that Dr Vause held up to his lips. Regina was at his side along with Mia who was tottering on the tips of her toes and fussing over the scruffy mane of hair that was protruding in all directions.

"Ruta." Tom tried to sit up straighter, everyone looked at me.

"Hey." I moved between my Aunt and the doctor and rested my hands on the sheet of the bed.

"How are you?" Tom asked flashing his fangs as he spoke.

"Better than you by the looks of it." I glanced down the bed, his frame was so narrow beneath the tangle of blankets.

"I'll be fine, wolves are supposed to be lean." He grinned.

"But humans aren't!" Regina chided.

"I want to come with you tomorrow." He said firmly.

"There's no way." I said cutting across the chorus of voices.

"I need to come with you." Tom stared at me.

"No way." I repeated. "Tom, this isn't going to be over in a day or so. We need you strong." I placed a hand on his shoulder, feeling the breath rattle through his chest.

"I'll be fine by the morning." Tom tried to press himself further up the bed wincing with the effort.

"You aren't going anywhere." Dr Vause placed his spectacles into the pocket of his white coat, he held a bag of clear liquid in his hand and carefully attached it to the tubing running from the crook of Tom's arm. "This will certainly speed up your recovery but if you try to move too soon, you will be back in this bed for quite some time." He stretched upwards and hooked the bag onto a small metal pin that protruded from the wall.

Tom huffed and slumped against his pillow, Mia stroked his hair tenderly.

"As soon as you are ready, join us." Regina patted his leg and stood up to leave.

"Regina, I think Mia should stay here when you leave." Tom said eyeing the witch nervously, she paused in her step.

"I agree." Regina nodded.

"But I want to come." Mia protested.

"It is no place for you. Greta stays as well." Regina said with finality and walked away, out through the heavy wooden doors.

"What about you? I bet you will be allowed to go won't you?" Mia asked looking in my direction. I shrugged and followed my aunt out of the room.

I paused on the spiralling stairs, the low hum of women's voices reached my ears I edged closer clinging to the wall.

"It's the right decision." I strained forwards, recognising Hannah's voice.

"I know. But it still feel's wrong bringing Ruta." Regina muttered.

"She is strong enough." I heard feet shuffling. "We need her to be with us. Marina will never believe that they are alive and well without at least one of them there, we don't know what state of mind she will be in."

"She would believe me." Regina's voice was quiet and I could hear the edge of worry tainting her words.

"Who knows? Nobody can know what she will be like by now after all this time." Hannah lowered her voice to a whisper.

"I'm scared she'll hate me." Regina's voice broke and was followed by a stifled sob.

"You're her sister. She won't hate you! When she hears how you have fought for those girls and all of the coven, she will be proud of you." Hannah's words were muffled. I moved forwards so that my face poked around the curve of the wall. Hannah's arms circled Regina's small body, her padded black jacket almost hiding the witches' face, Regina's pale hands rested gingerly on her waist. They stood there silently, I watched on not sure where to go, this moment was clearly an intimate one and if I was to appear now they would know that I'd been there the whole time. Hannah pulled back a little but kept one hand looped around Regina's waist with the other she raised her palm to the ivory skin of my aunt's face and rested it there, cupping the angular cheekbone, it was strange seeing the roles of power reversed this way, suddenly Hannah seemed the strong one.

"Ruta!" Mia banged through the doors behind me, I grimaced as both Hannah and Regina shot apart and turned their faces in my direction. Regina's violet eyes fixed on mine and narrowed a little.

"What?" I snapped turning to face my sister who flinched at the sudden movement.

"I was just going to ask if there's any way you can get Regina to change her mind and let us come with you. I really want to be there, you know, when they find her." She nudged her toe against one of the stairs nervously.

"No Regina is right, it's not safe and at least one of us should be here. If Greta is here with you then she can tell you what's going on. As soon as we get out of there safely, we will be coming straight back to the castle and you can be waiting for us." I pulled her into a hug. "I can't look after myself and worry about you can I?" I tried to laugh.

"But I am just going to be sat here worrying about you!" Mia cried, it was moments like this that reminded me why I always felt she was younger than me even though we were twins.

"Ruta, we need to start moving out." Hannah stepped down towards me her cheeks red and eyes on the floor. "You need to collect your gear and make your way to the courtyard."

"Yeah of course." I tried to catch her eye to smile but she looked past me to my sister who was rubbing her nose and sniffing back tears.

"Mia it will be fine. Ok?" She said gently.

"I'll see you soon, I promise." I told her moving away towards the corridor. "Be strong." She took a shuddering breath and tried to stand straighter, I turned and walked away.

"Hey wait up!" Hannah jogged to catch up to me and we fell into line padding across the flagged stone hallway our breath frosting on the air.

"What you saw, before....." Hannah began.

"You don't have to explain anything." I told her quickly. "I wasn't spying I just came out and didn't want to interrupt." Hannah smiled.

"No I know you wouldn't do that." She said quietly.

"It's nothing to do with me. I just want Regina to be happy." I shoved open the door to the dining hall and moved towards the piles of thermal clothes and back packs.

"I don't know what we will find in there." Hannah placed her hand on my arm halting me, she looked over her shoulder nervously to where Mr Bard was watching us with a cold stare. "Take this. If the very worst happens, don't let him turn you." She pressed a small black ball, smooth as a marble, into my hand. "You press the top where the groove is and throw it, it'll blow a crater in even a solid granite wall." She looked at me meaningfully and I nodded to show I understood what she meant. I would be better off risking my life to escape than suffer as a prisoner confined to the dark.

CHAPTER EIGHT

We moved slowly through the low hanging branches of fluffy conifers, crawling on our bellies across the hard ground avoiding the patches of snow. There were no words only the constant shuffling of bodies, my neck hurt from trying to look upwards whilst lying down, in front of me Regina and Sarro were slipping effortlessly forwards with barely a sound. The foot of the rock face came into view, the ground sloping up to meet its ruddy brown walls, we halted. Just as Tom had described it, a huge upturned tree protruded high up on the left, its roots exposed to the air, I strained my eyes but couldn't see the hole which had betrayed Vincent's eye. Regina waved a hand, indicating a low dip in the ground to our right, it curved sharply providing a hollow that would better hide us from view. I dug my elbows into the ground and followed the others, shimmying until I could roll into the space and tuck my aching legs beneath me.

"So everyone knows their job." Bard had insisted on coming with us and had dragged himself, refusing help so that by now he was red faced and sweating heavily, he wiped his brow and took a swig from a flask.

"Yes sir." Was the muttered chorus from the four hunters he had enlisted to accompany us. I smiled at one of them, a square jawed brute of a girl, her hair cropped close to her head and steel coloured eyes, she didn't smile back.

"Ruta, eat this." Regina slid beside me glaring at the girl who quickly looked away, she handed me a lump of something dark and sticky.

"Do I even want to know what that is?" I moved it from one gloved fingertip to the other.

"Probably not just eat it. It will give you a boost of energy." Regina grinned.

"You eat that." I pressed it back into her hand. "I'll eat this!" I pulled the zip on my jacket and reached inside to grab a pouch of high protein formula from the castle. My aunt huffed and shoved the mound into her mouth.

"What was that?" I frowned.

"Rabbit kidney and roseships with a little pinch of mint." She replied.

"I'm never eating anything you offer me." I told her firmly.

"Right." Bard shuffled forwards so he was in the centre of the loosely formed circle. "It's time to do this. We don't know what he has planned in there, or who is waiting, we thought that we had taken all of them out in the last battle or that at the least, the ones with any sense that had survived would leave the area, but we cannot be sure of anything anymore. So go carefully, cover each other stay up high when you can. Stealth is the key." He was addressing his hunters.

"What's the plan?" I whispered to Regina.

"Witches." My aunt addressed Sarro and two others that I didn't know so well, Tera and Willow. "Between the four of us we have a number of gifts that can be used to serve us well. Sarro can you still reach Greta?" We all looked at her strong angular face as it became still.

"Yes." She nodded.

"Good, depending how deep we have to go you may lose that contact." Regina began.

"Woah!" I spluttered, a few hisses quietening me rang out.

"What is it?" Hannah pressed her hand to my back.

"Sarro, when you just did whatever you did, I could feel you, in my mind." I was shaking slightly. "It was like you were in my ears just a whisper but the pressure was pushing against the back of my eyes."

"It's ok Ruta, that's how it starts." Sarro smiled.

"How what starts?" I gasped.

"You have telepathy." Regina was smiling broadly. "Of course you do!" She shook her head with a rueful grin. "You are your mother's daughter."

"I'm not sure I want telepathy." I cringed scrunching my eyes as a high pitched noise rang through my head.

"You can feel that?" Sarro was gawping at me.

"Yep!" I winced.

"Regina that is Greta coming through to me from over two miles away." Sarro was looking at me wide eyed.

"What does that mean?" I opened one eye.

"It means you have got a very powerful gift coming." Regina slapped my knee.

"Can I switch it off?" I rubbed my forehead as the ringing subsided.

"No, but you will learn to control it." Sarro told me encouragingly.

"So we head off." Regina continued "Sarro you will go first, you and Tera will lift the tree a little remember it's important that you keep listening for any sign of our enemies, keep low and out of sight if you can." Regina was looking up at the tree.

"Then my hunters will go in." Mr Bard interjected.

"Yes if it is safe to do so." Regina didn't even look at him but snarled none the less.

"Hannah you and Ruta follow last, Willow you cover the back of us, with your foresight and speed you will be the best placed to watch our retreat and our backs." Willow nodded and I noticed her eyes turn from a pinkish lavender to almost ice white. "Willow can pick up heat signatures, so if anyone tries to coral us she should be able to see which side they are coming from even if there is a wall in the way." Regina explained.

"Just remember, Marina will be confused, maybe not herself, do not harm her." Regina stared at the hunters one by one. "If she is harmed you will answer to me." Her voice was a growl.

"There's another gulley in the ground twenty feet that way." Hannah pointed to the left. "We can get there under the trees, but it means crawling again." Bard lay on his side and pulled a long bag from across his back. He unzipped it carefully to reveal a sleek ebony sniper rifle which he began to load.

"I will be watching. It's so dam overcast we can't count on sunlight to get them if they run." He crooked the weapon resting the barrel against the earth and moved onto his stomach to press his eye against the sight.

"Let's go." Regina motioned and silently exited the hollow.

Vincent bounced the rubber ball off the ceiling catching it quickly before throwing it again, he aimed for the face of a popstar on a faded ripped poster and flicked the ball forwards so it hit the smiling girl directly between the eyes before rebounding into his palm.

"Did you see that?" He laughed. Marina crouched in the corner her head down resting on bare scuffed knees. "I said did you see that?" Vincent launched the ball at the crown of her head, it smacked into her but still she didn't move. "What's wrong with you?" The vampire jumped to his feet covering the distance in two strides, he reached out gripping Marina's narrow arms and hoisted her off her feet. Her face was scarred with old wounds and new scrapes and bruises, but she smiled broadly.

"What have you got to smile about?" Vincent shook her violently. Marina laughed, cracking the rivets of dried blood that coated her cheeks.

"You should run." She whispered.

"Why would I run anywhere?" He growled.

A low barely audible rumble crept through the tunnel towards them making Vincent drop the witch and turn sharply. Marina crumpled to the floor. Vincent raised his dark head and turned his nose into the breeze, creeping forwards towards the shanty door and unhooking it from its latch silently.

"No!" He snarled.

"You are no longer a dead man Vincent." Marina struggled to her feet, the ragged sweater she had been given was ripped and loose around her thighs. She watched the vampire move across the space flipping over his camp bed he began digging into the earth furiously with an old can. The dust flew up into the air clogging her view, Marina squinted leaning forwards at the end of her chain.

"They will find me." She said with venom flinching as he moved through the cloud to within an inch of her face.

"I'm banking on it." For a second he smiled, Marina frowned, Vincent moved in a flash pressing a needle into the space over her heart and pressing down a plunger. Fire shot through her veins and she recoiled hitting the wall, the syringe stuck out from her chest, the faintest trace of black blood clinging to the tube. Her heart beat slowed, pounding in her head, the room span and she felt the earth beneath her body as she fell to the floor and took a shuddering breath. Her mouth opened to scream but no noise came out. She lifted her head as Vincent shot out of view, her body was so cold, colder than she had ever known, pain seared into every inch of her flesh becoming too much to bear and her mind lapsed into darkness.

CHAPTER NINE

The ground dropped away sharply, I pressed myself closer to the wall inching forwards, minute granules of soil fell from my shoulders. Ahead the hunters pointed the barrels of their rifles towards a sloping tunnel, the blue sights dotting the pathway, they signalled to each other and began to move into the shadows. I winced as a high pitched whine rang through my head, gritting my teeth I waited for it to pass but this time it didn't seem to be subsiding.

"Ruta." Regina whispered signalling me to follow. I stumbled forwards blindly, reaching out my hand.

"What is it?" Sarro held onto my waist and half walked, half carried me towards where the path widened.

"This pain." I tapped at my temple.

"You must shut it out." Sarro hissed. "Breath deep Ruta and focus on me." I forced my eyes open and gazed into the heavy lidded eyes of the witch who was inches from my face.

"Why does it hurt?" I gasped.

"It's a million subconscious words and thoughts pressing at your mind, I would be surprised if it didn't hurt." Sarro smiled tightly. "Now breathe and try to clear your thoughts, think of something calming or one face, think of the features the way it looks, smells and feels." I pictured myself resting my arms on the ledge of one of the castle windows, feeling the cold stone through my clothes, the wind pressing against my cheeks, the sound of the trees bending and swaying. The sharp pain subsided and I pressed myself to my feet.

"Better?" Regina whispered.

"Yes. Thank you Sarro." I said straightening my coat, I looked around at the cavernous hole we were in. "Are we inside the mountain?"

"Yes, one of the old passageways." Regina nodded.

"We need to move." Tera added stepping past us.

"Are you ok?" Hannah touched my arm as we stepped into the tunnel and began to climb upwards. I nodded. We squeezed into the space in single file, the hairs on the back of my neck prickling with every step.

"There's a door up here." I heard a man's voice call out followed by a loud snapping sound of splintering wood.

"Move back down." The broad shouldered figure of one of the hunter's came pushing towards us.

"I'm not moving anywhere." Regina spat and whipped through the gap, Hannah tried to follow but she wasn't small enough or quick enough to get past. We were shoved roughly back out of the passage and onto the rock shelf. Sarro snarled at the hunters who were gathering in a huddle blocking our line of sight.

"What can we do?" I asked Hannah quietly.

"We just have to wait." She shrugged. "If Regina gets into trouble she will call to us."

"Get out of my way." Regina slammed the man standing guard of the doorway into the wall and stepped into the blueish light of the torches. She squinted around the room before her eyes fell on the bundle of rags curled into a ball in the corner. A woman was trying to coax it to speak, Regina moved closer her heart hammering at her chest, the woman stepped back.

"Marina?" Regina croaked, the bundle moved slightly and a mop of dark hair lifted to reveal a narrow face, emerald eyes wide and searching.

"Gina?" Marina was shaking, her chin tilted upwards into the light showing the palette of bruising. Regina fell to her knees tears flowing down her face silently, her hands outstretched reaching tentatively towards her sister.

"Yes. Yes it's me." She whimpered.

"I never thought I would see you again." Marina's face crumpled and cracked as she leant into Regina's arms, the iron chain around her ankle rattled at the movement.

"Somebody get this off her." Regina commanded, shifting her weight onto her heels. A man squeezed past and within a few moment the metal was cut loose.

"Come on, we're getting out of here." Marina tried to stand, but her legs wobbled and buckled beneath her.

"It's ok." Regina braced her weight against her sister's side and slid an arm across her shoulders.

"It's not ok, none of this is ok." Marina sobbed. "I should stay here, you should just let me die."

"Don't say that!" Regina shook her fragile shoulders forcing her eyes to fly back open.

"Don't push me!" Marina snarled throwing out her hands sending her sister sprawling to the ground, the hunters instantly focused their weapons onto her, the blue lines crossing her face.

"No!" Regina scuttled forwards blocking their view. "Lower them!" Reluctantly they did. Marina was gawping at her hands in horror.

"I'm sorry." She spluttered.

"It's alright. After what has been done to you it's no wonder you don't want to be touched." Regina tried to soothe her but her own heart thundered with dread. "You should know something sister." Regina pulled her upwards and inched out of the room into the tunnel. "Your daughters survived."

"Both of them?" Marina gave a shuddering cry.

"Yes. We knew nothing of Mia until recently though." Regina started.

"He took her." Marina began to shake even more violently.

"We got her back." Regina said quickly.

"He tried to kill us all." The walls of the tunnel began vibrating, Marina's face had turned into a scowl, her emerald eyes darkening. "He tried to kill us all!" She bellowed, small stones tumbled from the ceiling.

"Marina! Stop this." Regina snapped giving her shoulder a heavy jolt so that her sister's famished frame was lifted a little off the floor, Marina blinked heavily and took a deep breath, the shuddering stopped.

"I'm sorry." She whispered again. They hobbled into the open, shuffling feet parting to allow them access, everyone fell silent.

I stared at the woman leaning heavily against my aunt. Her legs and feet bare and bloodied, caked with dirt and grime, her dark hair cut haphazardly protruding at sharp angles from around her face. She was looking from face to face, her eyes, just like my own glowing green in the dim light, she looked so small, so scared, nothing like the strong witch I had imagined. Hannah touched my hand and I jumped at the contact. The woman, my mother, flicked her eyes towards me at the movement. I thought it would be impossible for them to widen anymore, but they did, she groaned and slid to the floor never taking her eyes off me.

"Ruta, come here." Regina smiled through her tears.

"Ruta?" My mother sobbed, her hand outstretched wavering in my direction. I swallowed and stepped towards her. She pulled heavily on Regina's arm dragging herself upwards onto her feet, we were almost identical in height.

"It's ok." I told her as she reached for me.

"It's really you." I caught her by the forearms as she wavered, tears spilling down her cheeks. "You were so small when I last held you." She wrapped her arms around my neck and fell against me sobbing.

"I'm here now." I choked back tears.

"We need to get out of here." Hannah was looking nervously around. I pulled back.

"Can you walk?" I asked my mother tentatively.

"Not very well." She admitted.

"Here." One of the hunters laid a stretcher across the ground.

"Lie on this." We helped her onto the fabric of the sling and wrapped blankets tightly around securing her in place.

"I'll be right behind you." I told her releasing her hand and watching as she was whisked away.

"Something isn't right." Sarro mumbled. "She is different."

"Of course she is, wouldn't you be?" Regina barked.

"It's more than that." Sarro was undeterred. "Did you check her?"

"No! There is no need. She is my sister." Regina huffed and moved towards the hole that was our exit.

"Ruta." Sarro caught hold of my hand and looked at me hard. "Be careful."

"She's just weak." I said moving after the procession.

"No I mean it." Sarro pulled my hand so I turned to face her squarely. "Something isn't right." She emphasised the words. "Didn't you feel the very ground shake?" I opened my mouth to reply but Sarro continued. "Where is Vincent?" She arched an eyebrow. "Do you really think he would let her go so easily?"

"Maybe he got scared." I said carefully even though the words sounded hollow.

"He isn't the type to run off without leaving any kind of assault behind, even in cowardice he would still have prepared something for us, so my question is, if it isn't a trap of bullet or blade, what is it?" She looked pointedly towards where the stretcher was being pressed through the gap into the muted light outside.

CHAPTER TEN

The castle shone in the moonlight. I sat on the grass, my breathing deep and regular enjoying the silence. I rolled a piece of silver flecked gravel between my fingers and looked up at the leaded windows that flickered with candle light, I imagined the conversations taking place behind them. So much had passed since the last time I sat there, it was my favourite spot, sheltered by a swooping tree, the ground always kept cropped short with a rolling green stubble. I threw the piece of stone away and it bounced back to lie incognito with a million identical others.

"Hey." I jumped at the voice.

"Sorry." Tom pulled the blanket closer around his shoulders and held his hand up apologetically. "It's the wolf thing, I can't help it my feet just don't seem to make any noise!" I grinned and patted the floor beside me.

"Pull up a seat."

"Don't mind if I do." Tom wheezed as he bent down and dropped to the ground, he pulled a small plastic bag from a pocket in his khaki pants and unzipped it reaching inside with two fingers to pick out a squidgy dark lump.

"What is that?" I wrinkled my nose as he threw it into his mouth.

"It's goat." He smiled.

"Raw goat?" I baulked at the smell of blood. Tom nodded and reached for another piece.

"It's helping me, plenty of raw meat helps to repair my muscles." He flexed his arm to convey his point.

"Ok, I believe you, can you just eat it quicker." I turned my face away as he emptied the bag into his mouth and swallowed every piece. "That's disgusting." I added. He laughed and lolled his tongue out showing flecks of red.

"I am part animal." He stowed the bag away and rested his hands loosely over his knees.

"Have you seen her yet?" I asked.

"Nope." Tom sighed and looked up at the sky.

"It's only been a few hours I guess they have a lot of tests to do." I said.

"I don't know Ruta, in all honesty I haven't been down there to ask if I could see her." He shook his head. "What can I say?"

"I'm sure she'll be glad to see you and thankful you stayed with Mia the way you did." I told him.

"It's not enough. I should have known what he was doing." Tom ground his teeth in annoyance. "I should have tried harder to find the witches and tell them where she was. But I couldn't, I had no idea where the cavern was it was always kept a secret." He looked at me with earnest. "If I had left her to try and come to the castle or hunt Anise out they would have known something wasn't right and I never would have gotten back in. I couldn't risk her being alone. I had to try and wait until the time was right to get her out of there safely."

"Tom, everyone understands. It's more than enough what you did. You were her only comfort that makes you a hero to me." I leant my head against his shoulder. "You smell like a wet dog." I grinned at him.

"Thanks Ruta." He gave a small laugh. "But I still feel ashamed to stand in front of Marina."

"Come on. I'll come with you." I nudged at his ribs and pressed myself to my feet. "We can go together." I held my hand out to him, he eyed me cautiously before taking it and standing up. "It's not as if I have really spoken to her properly yet either, I need to take my own advice and get some courage."

"You are one of the bravest and most beautiful people I know." Tom cupped a hand under my chin. "Why do you seem so much older than Mia?" His amber eyes scanned my face.

"I don't know. We are definitely both twenty one but I can't guarantee how many seconds there is in it, maybe that makes the difference, maybe I'm slightly older." I forced a nervous smile. "We should go." I gently moved my chin out of his palm.

"I can't say no to that face can I?" He smiled and I felt myself reddening under his gaze. "Shall we?" He held out his arm crooked at the elbow and we moved towards the main entrance to the castle.

Dr Vause stood with his back to the wall, rubbing his glasses methodically in circles against his white coat. The double doors to his left housed small glass windows, I could see Regina's back as she stood at the foot of a bed.

"Ruta." He smiled softly and replaced the spectacles onto the bridge of his nose.

"Hi." I returned his smile nervously, Tom shifted from foot to foot looking as though he was about to be sick, all colour had drained from his face.

"How are you Tom?" The doctor looked him over critically.

"Fine." Tom managed to stutter.

"Can we go in?" I asked.

"Sure. Just try not to stay too long." He pushed open one half of the doors, the familiar smell of disinfectant wafted through the gap.

"Ruta." Dr Vause called my name quietly, Tom paused but I waved him in front of me, he grimaced and stepped towards Regina, I let the door swing closed.

"She won't let me examine her." The doctor began.

"It's probably because of whatever Vincent has done to her, she doesn't seem to like being touched. It's not surprising is it?" I was shocked by how defensive my tone was. He eyed me warily then nodded.

"Yes, of course." He smiled but his eyes drooped at the corners with sadness, the gnawing pain in my stomach pulled through my belly button like an invisible hook tugging hard. "Go on in." He held the door open for me once more.

"I can't believe it's really you." Tom was openly weeping, his head lying against the edge of the bed, my mother's hand rested on his scruffy tangle of hair, she smiled softly at him. Regina noticed me and briskly wiped away a tear.

"Ruta." My aunt came towards me her arms held out.

"Hi." I replied and accepted the embrace gratefully, I couldn't shake off the racing of my heart and she seemed to feel it. She held me away from her body, looking hard into my eyes.

"Are you ok?" She asked.

I nodded and forced a smile, it was all I could manage. "Has Mia been down here yet?" I added.

"No, not yet. I wanted to wait until you were here. I'm sending Hannah to find her now." Regina placed an arm around my waist and guided me forwards. Marina, my mother I reminded myself, sat upright against the stack of pillows, her hair had been washed and brushed, tidied into a short neat bob that barely brushed her chin. She was thin and clearly tired, heavy dark circles coated the hollows of her eyes, but the green of them seemed almost self-illuminating they shone so bright. The layer of dirt had been cleaned from her skin leaving a map of scars and fresh bruising, her lip bore a recent split at the corner that looked as though it would crack painfully if she were to smile. I frowned, the filthy sweat shirt still remained. She took a sharp breath as I came towards the bed.

"Ruta?" She asked. I nodded again. "They told me Mia might be coming I wasn't sure...." Her voice trailed away.

"Oh you'll know Mia when you see her." I laughed. "We may be twins but we are very different, I mean we do look almost identical, but she is definitely the sweeter one. Everyone loves her."

Regina smiled "As we do you." She told me.

"Why don't you let us get you some other clothes?" I asked. Marina's face flushed pink colouring the pale surface of her cheeks.

"I would rather just rest for the moment I'm sure I will be strong enough soon to dress myself, that will be something I haven't been allowed to do in a very long time." Regina caught my eye for a second and I saw my own fear mirrored in her lavender eyes. Something really wasn't right.

"I don't know why you keep looking at each other like that!" Marina spat, her eyes flickered and for a moment the green seemed to pulse with black specks. "I'm sitting here in front of you but you look at each other as though I were a child unaware of anything." Her voice rose up angrily.

"We are just worried." Regina said soothingly.

"Ruta?" A small voice called from behind me, I turned to see Mia tentatively poking half her body through the doors, a black velvet bow was neatly looped around the crown of her head matching her dress.

"Come in." I motioned her towards us, she eyed the woman in the bed nervously but stepped forwards.

"Mia." The name came out as a sigh. Marina shuffled up the bed her eyes bright filling with tears whatever anger had been there only moments before had vanished. Mia nodded and reached for my hand holding it tightly. We stood side by side a few inches from the bed, Marina looked between us.

"You are really identical, yet so very different." She whispered. Mia held out a piece of paper, she had drawn a vase full of brightly coloured flowers.

"I couldn't get real flowers for you so I tried to draw them." She pushed it gingerly onto our mother's lap. "It's not very good sorry." My sister stepped back and squeezed my hand pressing her body against my shoulder.

Marina lifted the paper in shaking hands and traced a finger over the grooves the nibs of the pencils had made.

"It is beautiful. Beautiful flowers like my beautiful girls." She held out her arms to us. "Come here." She pleaded. Mia burst forwards almost slamming into her chest and wrapped her arms around Marina's neck.

"Ruta?" Regina was at my side. "Go to your mother, its ok." She tried to guide me forwards but my feet remained rooted to the floor. My mother frowned and raised a hand to her temple, pressing at the skin below her hairline.

"I can hear him." I muttered.

"Ruta please, don't listen." Marina stretched her hand towards me.

"You hear it too?" I gasped as a searing burst of pain jolted across my scalp.

"Ruta?" Regina's voice was sharp it echoed around inside my head, my eyes fixed on my mother's as though welded in place. Through the chaos in my mind I could hear a cruel laugh, a man, his voice whispering, *she will always be mine.* My lips moved without me realising, I repeated the sentence over and over.

Marina's eyes widened as I stepped forwards reaching for a pair of scissors that sat on the surgical tray beside her. Before anyone could stop me I slid the blade through the front of the sweatshirt pulling the edges aside. All the noise stopped and suddenly the room came back clearly into focus. Mia had jumped away and stood behind me crying softly. I breathed heavily.

"It was before you came." Marina sobbed. I looked at the pale skin of her chest, in the hollow dip between her breasts was a black punctured hole and from it tangled under the skin spanned a web of purple veins. It wasn't the same as I had seen on vampires, it didn't spread up towards her throat, it seemed to wrap around the bones of her chest and congregate over her heart. The colour was definitely more of a purple than black and they were nowhere near as visible as a vampires should be.

"Marina what happened?" Regina's voice was shaking.

"He heard you coming, he pulled out a syringe, a needle full of blood...." She waved a hand towards her chest not finishing the sentence.

"Do you have a pulse?" I asked.

"Of course I do!" Marina barked her eyes flashing with the same blackness I had seen a few moments before, she rubbed her temples again hurriedly as though trying to shake off her agitation.

"You know what this means?" Regina looked at me. "They have finally created the hybrid of the blood lines they have always wanted."

"What's going to happen to me?" Marina asked gently.
Nobody had an answer.

CHAPTER ELEVEN

Vincent paced the edge of the clearing, his feet landing firmly avoiding exposed tree roots. The moon cast a white glow high above illuminating the small group of men who shuffled nervously keeping their leader within sight.

"She will find us." Vincent muttered more to himself than anybody else, he kicked aside a rotten log continuing his circle.

"Why would she come back when she has been reunited with the witches and those brats?" One braver member dared to question.

"Because the pull of my blood will be stronger than any of that!" Vincent shouted stopping and glaring into the huddle. "Don't you remember how it felt when you first shed your human skin? Don't you remember the pull towards the one who gave you your life?" He hissed.

"With all due respect sire, it was nearly two hundred years ago for me, I am not like yourself, a new born." The man who had spoken gave a grin to his companions.

"Time has no effect!" Vincent stepped forwards in one huge stride he was upon the man, fingers wrapped tightly around his throat, beads of black dotted where his nails pressed against the skin. "Maybe whatever creature turned you wasn't really fully blooded or maybe he was just weak and cowardly with blood thinner than water." Vincent threw the man to the floor and continued on his looping walk. "She will come to find me, for answers or revenge, but either way she will come and when she does the feeling will be more than she can bear, she won't want to be without me it will eclipse every other desire. Then, we will be more powerful than any vampire has been before. We will destroy Belladon castle and take rule of the information it holds, we will round up every last vampire in the world to create an army unlike anything you could imagine and wreak havoc on the humans who have held us captive in the dark for so long. With the mixture of blood we will be able to walk in the light! A new race will be born." Vincent grinned maniacally into the night sky his chest rising and falling with excitement. "She will come." He added with a laugh. "She has no choice but to."

Regina swirled the spoon around the wooden bowl pushing aside the crescent shapes of celery that floated in the soup. She looked up and around the cafeteria, the black and white floor tiles were scuffed and in need of a polish, marked from all the years of use, this is where it had all started, this place so different from the home she and Marina had shared as children, this is where Marina had met the twins father, one small moment in time and yet the world had changed because of it. She dropped her spoon into the bowl and leant back in the moulded plastic chair looking up at the ceiling.

"Hey." Hannah smiled as she came through the swinging doors.

"Hi." Regina replied sliding back into an upright position.

"So Dr Vause ran the tests." Hannah slipped into the seat opposite. "Her blood isn't like anything we've seen before." She reached out her hand and stroked the top of Regina's where a piece of cotton wool was taped in place. "It's not like yours and nothing like any of the vampire samples we have on record." Hannah sighed and reached for Regina's cup of water taking a sip.

"So what does that mean?" Regina asked.

"Well, the only things we know for sure are that she has a heartbeat, she isn't sensitive to light in a physical way but we think it may be affecting her mood, she seems to become much more agitated during daylight hours, almost like a over tired child, but more aggressive." Hannah gave another half-hearted smile.

"Is it black? Her blood?" Regina winced as she asked the question.

"No, it's not black. It's more like a plum colour." Hannah answered carefully.

"But it's not red." Regina tapped her fingers on the table top.

"No." She shook her head freeing the strand of honey blonde hair.

"So is she craving blood?" Regina's lip curled into a snarl.

"We don't know. In all honesty Dr Vause has been giving her a drip with a pint of deer blood in once a day, we had some in the stores as an emergency in case we ever needed to capture and hold a vampire and she hasn't rejected it. It's going directly into a vein and she seems to be doing well, there hasn't been any kind of incident." Hannah held up a hand to stifle the protest she knew was coming. "If she had rejected it we wouldn't have continued Regina, but as it is, she isn't showing any sign of craving human blood so as long as that continues then it's a good thing right?"

Regina nodded in defeat. They were right, no risk could be taken. "Has she stood up or been out of the wing yet?"

"No, she's sleeping a lot, her wounds have healed quicker than we thought they would though so it shouldn't be too long."

"Quicker than humanly possible?" Regina asked.

"Yes." Hannah nodded again.

"Life could never have just been simple for us could it?" Regina shook her head and lifted a hand to push back the dark locks of hair. "Those girls are so young and already they have been through more than they ever should have known. What else must they endure?"

"They are who they are. It's their life, their heritage and family. The same as it is yours, change that and you change who you are and the world just wouldn't be the same without the Ottoman women in it." Hannah smiled but Regina only looked on sadly.

"I'm not sure if that would have been for the better." She muttered.

A week floated past in a blur, I slept through most of it an insatiable tiredness lingered in my bones. In the waking gaps I practiced my telepathy with Sarro, passing messages to Greta who would run off to random places within the castle dragging Mia along with her and then wait for my mind to find hers. I visited my mother, who seemed to be returning to a more human form than vampire, we even were allowed to take her in a wheelchair to visit my grandmother's grave under cover of night when the students were in their beds.

"I always thought I would see them again." My mother sighed, her eyes held onto the sight of the headstone embellished with Sierra's name longer than Anise's.

"We didn't really get a chance to know her." I nodded towards the marble that bore my grandmothers name. "But we have heard plenty of stories." I smiled and glanced at Mia who stood solemnly fighting back tears.

"Oh she was one of a kind alright." Marina gave a short laugh.

"Sierra saved my life." Mia whispered.

"What darling?" Marina tried to turn around to look behind her but the chair limited her movements.

"She said Sierra died saving us." I repeated louder. "Mia got shot during the fight at Baron's cavern, we were trying to escape and she got shot through her ribs when the rescue was underway. She was gone I think, there was so much blood." I shook my head in a fidgety way trying to dislodge the image. "But Sierra pulled us under the staging Baron had built and she did something, some kind of incantation and the bullet lifted clear out of Mia's body then it all seemed to heal over and she woke up."

"But Sierra didn't." Marina lowered her eyes tears spilling onto her cheeks.

"Regina said she used her life energy and it took too much." Mia stuttered.

"Yes that sounds like something she would do." Marina lifted her head and turned her eyes back to the headstone. "Help me up please Ruta." She lifted her hand towards me and began to shuffle forwards.

I wrapped my arm around her narrow waist feeling the protruding bones and helped her step forwards before lowering her to the ground next to Sierra's grave.

"My beautiful girl." Marina held her palm out over the soil which shifted gently, my eyes widened as a cluster of snow drops lifted from the ground and unfurled to coat the edge of the stone, their heads whiter than the stars bowing against their stems. My mother touched one tenderly. "I always loved you, you know that, I don't know why I was blinded by him enough to ever leave you." She added stifling a sob. "Ok, I think it's time to return." She looked at me and held out her hand, I moved forwards and lifted her so that she clung to me for a moment. "Thank you Ruta." She whispered.

"It's ok." I replied.

"Don't think I don't see how strong you are, or how you have looked after your sister, because I do." She leant back and cupped my face. "But I am back now and our enemies will pay for what they have done." She turned from me towards the wheelchair, my heart thundering in my chest, her eyes, just for a second, had burned solid black again.

CHAPTER TWELVE

The bed sheets scratched at my bare legs, sweat coated my chest and forehead as I tossed from side to side conscious but unable to fully wake up. My mind was clouded with a muddle of voices, shadowy figures drifting through a petrol black fog their faces out of reach. I mumbled, hearing it echo off the walls of my room but still locked in my dream. The murkiness faded and he came clearly into view, Vincent, turning in the light his lips pulled back in a smile he held his hand out towards me crooking a finger and signalling forwards. I shook my head feverishly trying to back out of whatever nightmare I was spiralling into.

"Ruta!" Regina and Sarro barged into my room barely fitting through the door side by side. I heard them but could not lift my eyelids to open.

"It's a terror." Sarro's voice echoed around me, Vincent's hand recoiled to his side and he looked past me, I saw Regina reflected in his eyes.

"No!" I screamed at him.

I want her next, it won't be difficult she still loves me. His voice was smooth rustling past my ears like a breeze. *But now first things first, where is my queen?*

"Stay away!" My voice was loud but wavered.

"We need to get her out of there." Regina was pinning my flailing arms to the bed.

"She has to come out herself." Sarro held onto my legs as I kicked out.

"Is this real? Is she really seeing something or is it a dream?" Regina gasped.

"I don't know." Sarro grunted as my knee jolted her forwards.

Nothing can stop this Ruta, she is already on her way and because of that you will be too. You can leave the little one behind, she is of no real use to me. I want my new race to be strong and brave, not weak and whimpering. He grinned again as out of the milky clouds a woman emerged, her dark hair whipped back from her face, her eyes blazing green ringed by ebony. She reached for him pulling herself close to his body, blood coated her bottom lip, a stark contrast to the pale of her skin.

"Mother?" I questioned, the words barely left my mouth as an image of Marina running through the forest replaced Vincent's face, she flew, her feet barely touching down, her mouth set into a hard line of determination.

She is coming to me. Vincent's voice trailed off with happiness, my eyes shot open and I lunged forwards off the bed. Regina caught me as my knees hit the flagstones with a crunch.

"Ruta look at me!" She commanded, I flailed uncontrollably the words rushing over my tongue in a jumble of noise.

"Regina she is going to hurt herself there is no other way." Sarro barked.

"No! We need to know what she saw." My Aunt brought her hand up and slapped me hard across the face, I span to one side my ear ringing as I sucked in air. The room fell quiet, slowly I lifted my face I felt oddly calm all of a sudden.

"Thanks." I grumbled rubbing at my stinging cheek.

"I'm sorry but you were, out of sorts." Regina blushed slightly as Sarro fixed her with an unimpressed stare.

"I think I needed it." I told her moving to sit on the edge of the bed.

"Sarro felt a disturbance, anything strong enough to wake her up had to be pretty powerful. When we came in you were thrashing and shouting, what happened?" Regina moved alongside me wrapping a blanket over my shoulders.

"It was him, it was Vincent. He was talking to me, then he saw you, he said he wanted you and that it would be easy because you still love him." Regina hissed as I spoke. "Then my mother was there, but she didn't look like her, she was so strong and beautiful, there wasn't a mark on her and she had blood on her lips and black rings around her eyes, actually in her eyes around the green." Sarro looked to Regina with something like fear playing across her face.

"He said she was coming and I could see her running through a forest, so fast." I rubbed at my eyes, behind them felt tight and sore.

"Was it clear?" Sarro asked, I shrugged with confusion. "The images were they clear or hazy?"

"Oh, it was a bit like a fog." I answered.

"I'm going to the hospital wing." Sarro darted through the door, I turned to my Aunt.

"What a dream hey." I tried to laugh but Regina was shivering nervously, I waited knowing she would speak once she had gathered herself.

"I don't think it was a dream Ruta." Regina's lavender eyes fixed on mine. "The fact that it was foggy sounds like a vision, usually when somebody uses a soothsayer to make contact they do it by inhaling a mixture of poppy milk as the one with the magic chants the spell. Witches and other creatures with limited magical abilities used to sell their services to those who didn't have the means to make contact via telepathy themselves. It sounds like Vincent has done exactly that." Regina sighed heavily. "I should have made sure he was dead."

"But he can't actually get to me." I said carefully.

"Not physically." Regina didn't look up. "But if he can contact you he can definitely contact Marina and with her frailty, her mind being broken down by all the years of confinement…." She didn't get to finish the sentence before Sarro burst back in panting heavily.

"I just met Hannah coming up the stairwell." She drew in breathe. "She's gone. Marina is gone."

CHAPTER THIRTEEN

The closer she got to him the stronger her body felt. Marina paused to catch her breath, her hand rested against the trunk of a fallen tree cracked and snapped in the middle, the inside coated with fluffy green moss.

Not far now

Vincent's voice echoed through her mind as clear as if he was beside her but somehow still distant. She looked down at her legs, thin beneath the green cotton slacks she had taken from the castle, the smell of disinfectant clung to the fabric billowing up as she moved. Her head ached but she moved forwards not understanding how this creature had for so long kept her in chains and now even though she was free she could do nothing but return to him. She battled with the impulse to turn and head back the way she had come, looking over her shoulder down the path through the tree trunks.

I have the answers Marina, you will not find them anywhere else

She snarled as the voice pulled at her forcing her onwards, she struggled up an embankment stones rolling away as she kicked her feet into the soil and powered up the side emerging into the moonlight, muscles burning from lack of use for so long and sweat coating her body. A ring of trees crowned the top.

"You came." This time the voice was very real, Vincent stepped out of the shadows smiling broadly.

"I don't know why!" Marina lunged at him her fingers clawing the air as he skipped away.

"Yes you do." He laughed.

"No I don't!" Marina spat she rested her hands on her waist panting, sweat was trickling down her back cooling to a chill in the night air. "I can't understand why, after all those years of being chained up, I would choose to come back to you." She shook her head fighting the confusion.

"Because I'm part of you now." Vincent held his hands out as though welcoming an embrace. "My blood is in your veins Marina, there's no denying it, we are linked you and I. The further you pull away the harder it will become for you to exist, you would eventually drive yourself mad!" He smiled again. "We don't want that now do we?"

"I left my children." Marina sank to the floor her hands grasping at her hair. "It's ok, it's not as if it's the first time and they were fine before." Vincent moved closer. Out of the shadow of a thick set tree a small man had appeared, his hooded cloak hiding his features, he moved silently behind Marina a narrow glass vial clasped between gnarled fingertips. Vincent licked his lips and shuffled forwards a step more. "I mean maybe not totally fine, one was locked underground with my brother as his pet." Vincent smiled. "But she was never harmed at least."

"I didn't have any choice in leaving them and if he wasn't already dead I would kill him with my bare hands!" Marina roared. As she opened her mouth the old man popped the lid off vial and tugged her hair backwards tipping a dark wriggling cloud of liquid into her throat before leaping away with surprising agility. Vincent moved quickly back too.

"What the hell was that?" Marina grabbed at her throat, a dark mass moved under the skin snaking its way towards her heart, weaving beneath the web of veins spreading slowly outwards, the puncture wound on her chest closed over with unblemished skin, the bruises and marks on her arms and legs began to fade and blend into a flawless ivory palette. "What's happening to me?!" Marina looked at Vincent who was watching with awe. Suddenly she crumpled to the floor, a scream ripping through the air sending roosting birds flapping from their perch, she clutched at her chest, her lips quickly deepening to a dark shade of merlot. Her hair began to lengthen, black waves dropping past her shoulders shining brilliantly like polished jet. Marina tilted her head back gulping in air, her eyes burned as a dark ring pulsed around the edge of the emerald green orbs. "Why do I feel so feel cold?" She stuttered.

"That was the soul of one of the oldest vampires who ever existed." The old man crept forwards eyeing the unmoving woman carefully. "He was one of the founding fathers of your race. He knew that when the time came people would search for him and eventually kill him, his power was too much for them to ignore, so he used magic to ensure that his soul, the essence of his blood would endure. He had me remove it from his body and placed into this vial, protected by the strongest magic. You are lucky, not many could harness a power like his within themselves and survive it." He grinned toothily as Marina lowered her eyes and stared at him coolly. "Once it has been rebirthed it cannot be contained outside of a human body again, so you see the only way it can be destroyed is by killing the host. Take care of her Vincent or it will have been for nothing." The old man turned away and began to hobble through the trees.

"Marina?" Vincent moved closer and held out his hand nervously, but she took it and rose to her feet.

"Get me out of these clothes." She commanded in a voice that sounded stronger than her own ever had. Vincent clicked his fingers towards one of the watching vampires who hastily tugged at the drawstring of a jute sack loosening the top so that he could reach in and retrieve the pile of clothing. He approached with shaking footsteps, withering under the gaze of the woman who seemed almost unearthly in the moonlight.

"We will leave while you change." Vincent bowed a little and moved away. Marina flexed her fingertips eyeing them warily, the clothes consisted of a pair of leather trousers a thick woollen shirt and a heavy black velvet cape lined with silk. She reached upwards marvelling at how strong these arms felt, tugging the material over her head so that the night air wrapped around her bare skin, she pulled on the new outfit.

"You look beautiful." Vincent had reappeared.

"I know what you did to me, why do I not feel as though I should just kill you?" Marina frowned.

"Because you can see now that it was all for a reason. We will rule this world together you and I." Vincent cooed.

"I have daughters." Marina muttered. In the back of her mind images were flashing by, but somehow they didn't cause her any pain or emotion, it was like viewing somebody else's memories.

"Yes, the old part of you did. But you are new now, you are different, reborn." Vincent took her hand and held it firmly. "None of that matters anymore. None of them matter." He emphasised.

"None of it matters." Marina repeated quietly. "My veins feel as though they are burning." She scratched at her forearms.

"You need to feed." Vincent smiled. "Come on I know just the place for some fun."

He pulled at her hand and she followed skipping down the slope, hopping over rocks. A muffled crying reached her ears and she slowed sniffing the air, it smelt rich and irony and delicious.

"She's all yours." Vincent placed his lips near her cheek as he spoke and with one hand pushed her forwards to where a woman was bound to the trunk of a tree. A strip of dark cloth wrapped around her mouth, wedged between her teeth held her head back against the bark, exposing the pulsing vein of her throat, she struggled as Marina moved forwards. Blood coated her arms trickling down from a gash above one eye, Marina placed her mouth against it ignoring the frenzied whimpering of her prey and let her tongue catch a drip. It was more than she could bear, she ripped into the soft flesh without hesitation. The woman fell silent and still as her blood flowed freely from the sides of Marina's mouth.

"Enough now, you will gorge yourself." Vincent gave a light laugh and reached for the narrow shoulder. Marina pulled free snapping her head round to glare at him.

"I will decide when enough is enough." She hissed, but rose to her feet regardless, trailing the back of her hand over her mouth so that only a smudge of vivid red coated her lips.

"What now?" She asked.

"Whatever you want." Vincent stepped in closer. "There is a small village in one of the ravines, we could begin there. We will need to build up a small force to attack the castle."

"The castle." Marina's voice drifted slightly as she was bombarded by images of faces she knew but no longer carried feelings for.

"Yes we need the information from within." Vincent urged.

"So we start with the village." Marina nodded.

"Firstly though we need to give your blood to the followers we already have." Vincent spoke quietly, the vampires half hidden in the trees began to shuffle forwards.

"My blood?" Marina narrowed her eyes.

"Yes, you carry the blood we need to be able to walk in the light and to make the most powerful race of vampires there has ever been, you will be the queen, the founder of a new generation." Vincent spoke hurriedly, his excitement clear. He picked up Marina's hand and twisted it softly over to reveal the underside of her wrist where a dark splayed vein was visible.

"I wish to be the first." He lowered his face to the skin keeping his eyes on the woman's above, he hovered his mouth waiting for her approval which came in the form of a barely noticeable nod. With a short grin he sank his teeth in, sealing his mouth around the wound. Marina frowned, her lips pulled back in a snarl but she resisted the urge to move away. A moment passed, barely a minute before Vincent moved his head away. His eyes now gleamed a pale jade green. Behind him a line had formed, each man eager to take his turn. "I feel unstoppable." Vincent giggled. "This feeling is like nothing I have ever known. The power, nobody can stop me, this is my world now I am a king!" He jumped to his feet and grabbed Marina's face, pressing his lips to her own. She reacted instantly.

"You are no king! You never will be any kind of master to me again. My master is within my veins and he is more powerful than anything on this earth. He is reborn within me and he doesn't like you very much for the things you have done to me." Marina pouted in mock upset. "You will never know what it is like to rule." She threw Vincent backwards his eyes wide as he soared through the air before pummelling the floor, she held out her hand, a black mass of muscle sat in the palm, tubes dangling limply, leaking inky blood into the soil. "Even you can't come back from a ripped out heart." She snarled throwing the organ to the floor before turning back to the line of men and barking, "Who's next?"

CHAPTER FOURTEEN

"We found the trail." Hannah announced as she strode into the dining room.

"And?" Regina was on her feet.

"We found Vincent." Hannah sighed sitting beside me in front of the fire.

"Where is he?" I asked.

"Dead." Came the reply.

"I wanted to kill him myself!" Regina fumed moving around to face Hannah.

"He was dead when we got there." Hannah answered sharply. "His heart was ripped out." I looked at my Aunt who was as dumbstruck as myself.

"So who killed him?" I asked.

"I don't know Ruta." Hannah rubbed at her eyes tiredly. "But it was a clean wound, in and out."

"Did you find Marina?" Tom asked from the corner of the room where he was curled up quietly on a chair.

"No, but we found the clothes she had taken from here. We found her tracks leading up to where Vincent was, we found the small camp they had been using for a few days we found tracks of at least ten other vampires and a man." She frowned. "He left on his own though, sometime before the others, one of the hunters is following his trail as we speak. But no, we didn't find Marina."

"The soothsayer." Regina added grimly.

"I think so." Hannah nodded in agreement. "If we can locate him we may be able to find out where Marina is and if Vincent had anyone else of significant power working with him. I mean there has to be some kind of plan in place, because otherwise where would they be?" The words hung in the air, all of us felt the weight of them.

"Was there any other casualties?" I asked.

"Yes, a woman, a human. She had been bound and gagged, bitten but drained of blood, not kept alive. There was only one bite wound though, the mouth size seemed like that of a woman's." Hannah spoke the last part very quietly and stared into the flames not making eye contact with either myself or my aunt.

"Whatever has happened, somebody must be withholding my sister or else she would have returned to us after Vincent's death." Regina stated firmly.

"Unless she doesn't remember who she is anymore." Tom muttered.

"Impossible! She has only just found her freedom and her family again. She is stronger than that." Regina shouted.

"Regina, I think Tom is right. The tracks leading away, well, they were led by a woman." Hannah looked up nervously.

"I will not believe that my sister would turn to any kind of darkness." She screamed. "This is your mother we are talking about Ruta have you nothing to say?"

"I don't know what to say." I admitted. Regina glared from face to face in disbelief before storming from the room. Tom squeezed himself from his seat and silently moved in front of the fireplace where both Hannah and I were staring blindly into the flickering flames.

"So what do we do?" He murmured scratching behind one ear.

"What can we do?" I sighed. "She hasn't come back, Vincent is dead, we don't know where this band of Vampires has gone or if they are holding her captive. I mean, they have to be holding her don't they?" I looked at Hannah.

"Ruta there was no sign of any struggle, your mother left here of her own free will and went to Vincent out of choice." She looked at me with sadness. "Whatever has happened I think we need to start coming to terms with the fact that Marina isn't the same person she was all those years ago and she probably won't ever be again."

Tom paced away giving a low growl, something between anger and sadness that whittled away into a whine. The room fell silent, a lean wolf loped from the corner and scratched at the door he turned and looked towards us.

"I wish you would give me some kind of warning before you do that." Hannah scolded as she opened the door allowing Tom to exit the room.

"I don't understand." I shook my head. "All those years of being held against her will and as soon as she is even slightly strong enough to leave us again, she does! Maybe we got it wrong, maybe she wanted to be with him."

"Ruta I don't think that's true." Hannah tried to calm me down but the anger was flooding over me.

"We haven't got a clue what she really wants, but it obviously isn't me or Mia." I was shouting now. "I heard him too! He didn't threaten her or us, he didn't give any kind of ultimatum that was impossible for her to turn away from. He whistled and she went running!" I stood up and kicked out at the table which barely moved infuriating me further.

"Ruta, the pull he will have on her now will be almost unbearable. You know that, you have learnt all about the symptoms that follow when a vampire is created." Hannah tried to reason with me.

"Is that what she is now then? A vampire?" I yelled. "Because nobody seems to know exactly what we are dealing with or if there is any humanity left in this woman we are trying to save. Maybe we should let her go, maybe there's no point trying to reason with somebody who doesn't want to be with us." A heavy object slammed into my back sending me sprawling across the floor, I wheezed in small gulps of air, my chest constricted from the fall.

"Regina!" Hannah shouted. I turned to see my aunt looming over me her hair tussled and eyes shining wildly.

"You should be ashamed of yourself." She spat. "Is this how you behave when you are faced with a problem? You resort to whining like a baby and doubting one of your own?" She recoiled in surprise as I pressed myself to my feet ignoring the pain shooting through my chest.

"She isn't one of my own." I growled. "She left us once and we gave her another opportunity and she did it again. She is nothing to me!"

"Ruta be careful what you say next." Regina's voice was deadly calm. I eyed her warily biting back the torrent of hateful words building in my throat. "You are upset, I understand that, but some things cannot be taken back, remember that." She added.

"You're right." I said holding eye contact with her even though I trembled. "A lot of things can't be undone or taken back can they?"

"Meaning?" Regina challenged me, stepping closer to my face.

"Maybe none of this would have happened if you hadn't been so blinded! Or maybe you just didn't want to see it!" I screamed, tears streaming down my face.

"Say what you mean." Regina almost smiled.

"If you had paid more attention you might have seen what he was hiding! You left me here on my own, thinking I had nobody, that all my family were dead! Mia, was left being raised by a horde of vampires never seeing daylight. While you flounced around in love. Maybe you should have looked a little bit harder at the person you were lying back and sharing your bed with." I heard the slap before I felt it. I gasped as time seemed to slow down, my feet lifted off the floor, the entire front of my body tingled with a steady stinging sensation, Regina was frozen in motion the palm of her hand held out in front of her with a cloud of shimmering light billowing outwards around me, her eyes narrowed but blazing in the light. I twirled around, the air felt heavy like moving through water, I used my arms to manoeuvre my body out of the flow of light and placed my feet onto the floor. A small pop sounded and the air became lighter again, my legs felt like lead, Regina lowered her hands and span around looking across the room.

"What the hell just happened?" Hannah exclaimed.

"There's only one person I know of who can slow down time like that on command and so well practised." Regina looked abashed.

"I would say that, that, is quite enough." A clipped English accent from almost directly behind my head made me jump.

"Aunt Seraph." Regina flopped into the chair staring sullenly at her feet.

"Who else?" A woman stepped out of the corner of the room, a brown fur coat wrapped around her shoulders, her dark hair pinned up into curls that were tucked neatly on one side under a red beret. She looked entirely like she had just stepped out of the nineteen fifties. "And not a moment too soon by the looks of things." She pulled off a pair of long silk gloves and held out a porcelain white hand to me. "How charming to meet you." She smiled through crimson painted lips.

"You too." I shook the hand briefly, stepping aside as she strode past and tugged open the velvet curtains letting light flood the room.

"Well." She looked at Regina. "Are you going to explain what is going on or shall I guess?" Regina opened and closed her mouth several times unable to find the words to begin. "Oh, never mind." Seraph said briskly and came towards me once more. "I will find out for myself." She clasped her hands either side of my head pinning me in a vice like grip, I tried to protest but found myself struck dumb, unable to either move or speak. After a minute the woman broke free, her hands trembling.

"Regina. You should have sent for me!" She mumbled grasping onto the edge of the long dining table.

"I didn't know where you were and by all rights you should be an old woman by now." Regina ignored the look both Hannah and I cast her way.

"Yes I suppose that is fair comment, I didn't leave on the best of terms." Seraph conceded.

"How old are you?" Hannah asked.

"Well, young lady that is not a polite question, but I will say that Anise was my younger sister." Seraph gave a dazzling smile.

"How is that possible? You don't look older than fifty." I flinched as she huffed in my direction, Regina barely stifled a laugh.

"Many things are possible when you know how." Seraph said testily. "You are definitely your mother's daughter, Marina always lacked any tact too."

"I am nothing like her." I said quickly. Regina began to speak but Seraph held up her hand.

"Let the girl have her moment of anger, she's earned it I'd say." She pursed her lips and watched me carefully over the top of a cigarette that she lit and delicately pulled on. "You can rage against it all you want, you cannot deny the blood in your veins as much as Marina cannot deny the new liquid coursing through hers." She blew out a cloud of smoke. "I understand your anger, because I've seen your pain. But think for a moment if you can, of how your mother must be feeling right now." I opened my mouth but the hand raised once more commanding my silence. "I have seen her through your eyes, so you can't pretend that you don't see her weakness, her broken spirit and damages of the mind." I lowered my eyes to the vintage rug spreading across the floor. "Then atop the heartache and torture that she must have endured, she has a dose of something so powerful forced upon her that it can rip her away from everything she holds dearest. I would say that she is probably terrified right now and not at all in her right mind. In fact I have the strong feeling that somebody entirely separate is in her mind." She flicked a bead of ash to the floor.

"What do you mean?" I asked.

"Well, this Vincent character is dead, but still she hasn't returned to us." We all nodded. "That to me seems odd in itself, of course the pull to a maker is unbearable, but should that person no longer exist then surely the pull should not either?" I frowned. "So it stands to reason that perhaps whatever has happened to our dear Marina, somebody else is now pulling the strings?"

"Hold on, Hannah you said that the human tracks left the clearing before the vampires did?" I said.

"Yes definitely, it must have been the soothsayer." Hannah confirmed.

"And Vincent was still alive then, because his footprints crossed over that path?" I muttered.

"Yes." Hannah agreed.

"So something happened between him leaving and Vincent dying." Seraph clapped her hands together.

"We need to find that man." I said grimly. "It's the only way we are going to get any kind of answers."

Seraph rose to her feet. "Shall we?" She held out her arm to me crooked at the elbow.

"Where do you want to go?" I queried.

"Well I dare say that we are off up amongst the mountains and I can't possibly accompany you in these, they are vintage chanel, it would be a crime to subject them to such terrain." She lifted a foot to show the caramel coloured sling backs. "So I need to be appropriately dressed if you please." Hannah gave a grin that was mirrored by my own.

"This way m'lady." I gave a mock bow and smiling despite myself headed out of the room.

CHAPTER FIFTEEN

I adjusted the leather straps of Matisse's saddle and patted his neck with my free hand, Aunt Seraph had taken over as his passenger so I was reassigned to one of the youngsters. Matisse swung his head around to where I was standing and eyed me with his big liquid gaze.

"I know, but what can I do?" I smoothed the palm of my hand over his ear, he lowered his head and pressed it into my side nudging me playfully.

"He will be quite alright with me." Seraph appeared pulling on her leather gloves and striding across the gravel, she looked so different dressed in the fitted black trousers and heavy padded jacket, a woollen cap pulled down over her ears, ebony curls poking from beneath. Matisse shifted his weight and I smiled as he rolled his eyes. "Yes I remember you too foaly!" Seraph said as she swung herself nimbly up into the saddle. "We go back quite a way." She busied herself adjusting the bands of plaited leather.

"Foaly?" I grinned at Matisse who snapped his teeth in the air.

"Oh yes. I have known this boy since before he was born. Are you pleased to see me?" She leant forwards and tickled the tops of his ears laughing as he shook his head in annoyance.

I turned away from the procession and moved along the line towards the thick stone steps of the castle. Mia stood solemnly, twisting her gloves between her hands, she watched me approach with tear filled eyes.

"It will be fine. We will be back in no time." I told her.

"I should be allowed to come, I'm the same as you." Her voice shuddered with the effort of holding back tears.

"No you're not." I smiled "You are much nicer."

"I'm just as strong." She pouted.

"Yes you are. But one of us needs to stay here, to keep an eye on everything. It's really important because if any information comes in from the hunters you can get Greta to pass it to us straight away. If you weren't here how would we ever know?" I told her sternly. "Besides, if the very worst did happen, which it won't, but if it did, you would be the last Ottoman witch and could carry our line on." I patted her shoulder gently. "You have to be brave now Mia." I told her.

"I will." She nodded her head and tears fell down her cheeks.

"I will see you really soon." I smiled and turned away with a sinking feeling in the pit of my stomach.

"He's over there." Hannah called out to me as she nudged her horse forwards following the slow moving line of people in front. I craned my head to where a leggy chestnut colt was straining at his halter attached to a frightened looking young girl. His eyes widened and nostrils flared as he let out a neigh that shook his entire body and pranced to the side.

"His name's Conker." Regina moved alongside me atop a stunning black mare, her legs dangled loosely around the horses' body and she held the ends of a frayed piece of rope in her hands which attached to a makeshift bridle.

"Who's this?" I stroked the satin shoulder of the mare.

"This is Aura." Regina smiled proudly at her steed.

"So Seraph gets Matisse, you get Aura, Hannah gets Solstice and I get Conker?" I frowned watching as the youngster stumbled over his own feet, snorting at the rope.

"Yes." Regina nodded and with a laugh trotted away down the drive.

"Great." I sighed and moved closer to my new mount.

"Here!" The girl shoved the rope into my hands and darted out of the way.

"Ok, hey you need to chill out!" I told him sternly, to my surprise the animal stopped pulling and looked at me with eyes on stalks. "We are going to be spending a lot of time together so we need to trust each other." I added. He cocked his ears and nickered softly. "I know your eager to follow your friends but if you rush into things you're going to get us both hurt, do you understand?" Unbelievably, he bounced his red head up and down in a nod.

"Right, well, let's get started then." I said pressing my foot into the stirrup and hopping up into the saddle, every muscle in his body twitched eager to move. "Two seconds ok?" I muttered altering the many straps. "Ok, we can go." The words barely left my mouth before he bounded forwards in a strapping trot that covered the ground effortlessly, pulling up alongside Aunt Seraph who was at the front.

"Oh hello." She smiled. Matisse gave a nip to the younger horse who dutifully fell back a step.

"This horse is crazy!" I exclaimed pushing my hair from my face and bumping up and down as Conker jogged on the spot, Matisse planted his feet and firmly swung his head round landing his teeth in the chest of the youngster who gave a frightened squeal, hard enough to pinch but not break the skin. Instantly Conker slowed himself, lowering his head meekly and walking calmly.

"Well he just got told off by his daddy so hopefully he should be slightly better behaved now." Seraph laughed as Matisse moved forwards with a snort.

"Matisse is his dad?" Seraph nodded at me. "Well that figures."

"So, while we have this time together why don't you tell me about yourself?" Seraph reached into a pocket on her jacket and pulled out a long white cigarette, placing it between her lips she removed a glove and snapped her fingers together so that a pale blue flame appeared at the tips. I gawped as she waved her hand extinguishing the fire.

"How did you do that?" I asked.

"Oh merely a trifle." She shrugged "Tell me about yourself." She blew the smoke upwards, Matisse gave a rumbling neigh. "Oh shut up I've done it for years!" Seraph hissed.

"Well, there isn't much to tell really. I came here as a kid, nothing really happened until recently and then you know the rest and here we are." I said.

"No boyfriend?" Seraph grinned.

"NO!" I flushed red.

"Why not?" She frowned.

"I don't know I just never really thought about it." I said truthfully. "It's not allowed at the castle, we aren't supposed to have any relationships."

"What a ridiculous rule." Seraph scoffed flicking the ash to one side.

"I don't know, it makes sense really, you never know what's coming do you." I sighed.

"Exactly." Seraph smiled again. "That is why you should live life to the absolute fullest, what is the point of living if you can't love? Life without love is merely an existence, don't ever settle for just existing Ruta." She reached across and clutched my hand for a moment squeezing it.

"Do you have a boyfriend?" I asked.

"Oh several." Seraph replied. I laughed loudly making Conker spring forwards a step. "I have lived a very long time and in a huge variety of places, it would have been selfish of me to keep all this to myself." She waved a hand over her body and pouted.

"Don't take any advice from her Ruta." Regina had moved up behind us and was grinning.

"Oh you can talk!" Seraph slid around in her seat. "How many boys did we have to turn away from the woods when you and Marina were younger? All summer long, those two would make a habit of appearing next to the camp sites, bathing in the lakes and driving the young men wild. For days after we would see them rambling through the trees, searching for the fictitious camp site that was on the other side of the mountain where the two beautiful girls were staying. Always the same eager questions *'do you know them? They have jet black hair? She kissed me!'* Your mother and I would have to point them back to the trail telling them the girls have gone home, to get them to leave." Seraph wagged a finger.

"We were young and it was Marina doing the kissing not me!" Regina said indignantly.

"Oh I remember well young lady, you cannot fool me!" Seraph turned back in her seat and winked at me.

"Those days are long ago now anyway." Regina's smile slipped "They will never be again."

The trail petered out into single file, curving through the trees, giving way to long stone slabs that jutted from the earth. The entrance to the cavern was as well-hidden as it always had been, draped in heavy curtains of ivy and moss.

"I can't believe I am back here." Seraph sighed as we passed through into the darkness, the horses' hooves echoing off the walls.

"It's only for the night." I tried to sound sympathetic.

We shuffled forwards onto the ramp, I gritted my teeth as the giant rock groaned and began to lower into the light of the main cavern where a crowd of witches were waiting eagerly to take the reins of the horses.

I jumped down and gave Conker a pat. "Good boy." He nickered in reply and moved away with the others towards the holding pens that were stacked with fresh straw and hay.

I looked around, breathing in the familiarity.

"Nothing's changed has it?" I smiled at Seraph who had turned pale in the watered down light.

"Everything has changed." She whispered. "I didn't think it would feel like this, coming back here, but it is almost too painful to bear."

"Seraph, you can take my quarters." Regina signalled towards the corridor that was lit with stubs of waxy candles.

"Thank you Regina, I believe I need to lie down for a while." Seraph moved away from us quickly disappearing from view.

"She and Anise had a huge argument before she left." Regina explained. "Over a man. Seraph wanted to bring him into the coven, Mother wouldn't allow it of course. She didn't trust him." Regina gave a hollow laugh. "When she had returned to us to ask if he could accompany her here and live in the cavern, she hadn't explained to him where she was going, he knew nothing of what she really was or where she was from, he thought Seraph had left him, he believed she must have another man at home, a home that she wouldn't discuss with him but had to return to every few weeks. So, in anger and believing she was gone, he joined the army at the outbreak of the second World War."

"Oh no." I knew what was coming. "He didn't come back did he?"

"No, he was killed within a week by German infantry, Seraph never forgave mother. They had a blazing fight that nearly brought half this place down and she left to return to London. I think that is partly why mother allowed Vincent in, she was afraid it would happen again. She perhaps should have trusted her instincts." Regina lowered her eyes.

"So has Seraph never been back here since then?" I asked.

"No." Regina shook her head. "I think she stayed in London hoping that maybe it had been a mistake and that he would eventually return to her. She changed areas, altered her name and appearance somewhat so that if she came across someone she had previously known they wouldn't marvel at her unchanging appearance. But it's just a glamour spell, underneath is still the same."

"So is that how she looks so young still?" I queried.

"Not exactly, how you see her now is how she actually is." I frowned. "If a witch doesn't use a lot of her magic over the years, it can almost pool and form a supply well. The more you use, the more effort it takes, the higher drain it places on the body." Regina explained. "So Seraph, living a normal life hasn't used her magic almost at all." I nodded to show I was following. "So she taps into it and uses rejuvenation spells that repair the body. I mean her magic is very strong, she is after all one of the oldest witches of our line and we are renowned for the level of magic we possess. She stops when she gets the desired affect she wants, therefore keeping herself at a certain age physically."

"So could she keep going until her magic ran out? She could reverse time and be a kid again!" I exclaimed.

"No, it only repairs the body to the original state of when she started using the spell. I think she was about fifty five, therefore each time she applies the spell her body returns to how it was at that time." Regina looked at me with amusement. "Do you understand?"

"Yes." I nodded. "That is really cool though."

"Yes I suppose it is, but also very sad I think." I cocked my head unsure what my Aunt meant. "She is still hoping, don't you see?"

"I do now." She was still waiting for her lost love, holding onto a glimmer that he may return one day and recognise her.

"Regina, the hunters have arrived back, they found the trail of the man, we were right he was a soothsayer." Hannah bustled up to us.

"Was?" Regina turned her head.

"Yes. He was dead when they found him." Hannah nodded, holding her hands out in despair. "It looks like he had been living up on the mountainside in an old cave for decades. There were scrolls and scores of potions and bottles."

"We need to go there." Regina lowered herself onto the log in front of the ever burning fire pit. "There might be something."

"Tomorrow." Hannah agreed. I joined them on the make shift seat, holding my hands out into the glow. My stomach churned in the silence, a wave of anxiety striking back and forth inside me.

"How did he die?" I asked.

"His heart was ripped out." Hannah looked at me sternly, I understood what she wasn't saying I felt it settle on me like a weight. We needed to find Marina, fast.

CHAPTER SIXTEEN

The body of the man had been covered with a blue plastic tarp, weighted down at the ends with a few loose rocks. I stared at the outline of him, lying motionless, it didn't seem real, everyone was walking past him talking and picking up items to examine, objects that he had kept ordered and in their chosen places. I wondered if he would be angry now watching his things being handled and moved about. The wind fluttered his covering billowing up so that a corner tugged free flipping back to expose his pale face, eyes wide and staring with pupils that were clouded milky white. I fell back a step in horror at the sudden exposure of his features, the bundle on the floor suddenly became a person, but nobody else had seemed to notice. I looked across the cave, Regina was hunched over a roll of paper, Hannah at her side they were pointing out lines and following them with their fingers. I bit my lip and edged forwards, I would have to recover him. Dropping to my knees, I leant carefully closer reaching for the curling corner of plastic trying desperately to avoid touching any of his skin. I flicked my eyes to his almost apologetically but froze as I looked at the shining orbs. They were swirling with colour. Like marbles in the light, strands of pink and blue were racing across the white surfaces. I opened my mouth to shout to my Aunt but crumpled as searing pain burnt the backs of my eyes turning me blind. I felt the scream lodge in my throat but heard no sound, scrambling backwards on my heels plunged into a world of darkness, I kept scuttling along until I felt something hard at my back and could go no further.

"What is happening?" I screamed, reaching my hands to my own eyes I felt to make sure that the lids were open, my fingers brushed my lashes and I groaned as I confirmed that they were. I blinked hard trying to control my breathing.

"Regina!" I shouted to no reply. "This can't be real, someone would have noticed me by now." I rationed out loud in the silence. "Have I gone deaf?" I began to panic, then realised I could hear my own voice and the scuffling of my feet.

"You are not really blind." A man's voice close to where I sat made me jump.

"If I lift the darkness can you be counted on not to run? The last time I did this the young man ran blindly straight off the edge of this cliff." The voice sounded old, warbling in tone.

"Yes. I won't move just please tell me what is going on." I splayed my hands either side of my body rooting myself into the earth.

"Remember, I am no more substantial than air. I cannot stop you or help you if you choose to flee. I do not have any desire to hurt you or see you hurt I merely wish to speak with you." The darkness was lightening, I blinked rapidly as the cave came back into view.

"You're dead!" I gasped as an old man, the same one whose body lay only a few feet away, came into focus, he was seated in a wooden rocking chair before me, smiling serenely, his eyes a crystal blue.

"Yes, unfortunately I have to agree, I am dead." He nodded looking over his shoulder to where his corpse lay. "But I have had as they say, a good innings." He smiled wider.

"Where is everyone?" I looked around, apart from us and the man's former self, the place was empty.

"Oh they are still here. But they are in the present. We are on another plane." He explained.

"Ok so how do I get back?" I could hear the panic rising in my voice. "Can I get back?"

"Of course." He reached for a small metal cup that was filled with a steaming clear liquid. "I do miss tea." He sighed.

"Can't you drink it?" I asked.

"No, I don't have a body anymore, where would it go?" He laughed a low chuckle.

"I don't mean to be rude, but how and why am I here with you?" I sat up straighter.

"Of course." He replaced the cup and leaned forwards in his seat. "You asked me a question so I had to answer and the only way I could do that was to bring you here."

"I don't understand." I shook my head.

"When you looked into my eyes, well the eyes of that withered hunk of flesh." He shoved a thumb behind him towards his lifeless body. "You asked me, who did it." I stared at him dumbfounded, that question had been in my mind as I had attempted to re-cover his face.

"You didn't know you were able to commune with those on a different plane?" He asked.

"No." I muttered.

"Ah, well that is why it only happened when you looked into my eyes then." He tapped a hand on his leg. "With practice you should be able to do it without the presence of the body."

"What, close my eyes and talk to the dead!?" I scoffed.

"Yes exactly, well those who wish to be spoken with anyway." The old man nodded his head. "You must be careful though and only search out the exact person you are looking for. It is safer to do it this way, by direct contact, but not very pleasant I imagine."

I scratched at my head, it felt sore at the back.

"Well in answer to your question, I believe I have some explaining to do." The old man was frowning down at his feet. "And to do that I must go back quite some way. I was once servant to an extremely powerful vampire, he was one of the very first vampires in existence actually and his name was Michael. He wielded his power and bloodlust in terrible ways, wiping out whole families, even tiny babies. Of course this kind of behaviour got him quite a reputation and over the years many a gallant man tried and failed to kill him. As time passed though and technology advanced, Michael realised that he would eventually be overthrown, he could not continue on forever nor do I believe he wished to. He was cruel enough as a human and unbearable as a vampire, nobody could remain in his presence I only stayed because I was too terrified to leave. The loneliness affected him though, it turned him sullen almost depressed if you can believe it." The old man looked at me and licked his lips nervously. "He injected himself with an ultra violet solution, I have no idea where he acquired it from, but it gave him a day or so to live, an awful thing to watch, his flesh seemed to rot and burn away inch by inch. Just before his body gave out, he had me transfer his soul, his essence or whatever you want to describe what lurked inside him, to a magically protected container, a plain glass vial that would blend in amongst normal potions. The spell was such that it could remain intact within its containment until released to once again live and breathe within another body. He wanted to return at another time you see, when things may be different and people had forgotten him."

"Did Vincent take the soul?" I asked.

"No, I am afraid for you it is worse than that." The old man looked up sadly. "I am ashamed of what I have done, you must understand that." He pleaded.

"Go on." I said, my voice cracking.

"It could only be placed in a person who bore strength enough to hold it. Not physical strength you see but strength of character, of heart, someone who would survive almost anything." He whispered.

"Someone who could survive near death, survive the loss of her children and her freedom." I muttered placing my face into my hands.

"Yes." He agreed in a whimper. "I placed the soul into your mother." I looked up at him, tears dotting my eyes. "I am so sorry." He almost cried.

"So what happened?" I asked.

"He has taken hold of her." The man shuddered. "She killed Vincent, she killed me so that I wouldn't be able to tell anyone of what is to come but she obviously wasn't aware of her daughter's gift."

"What do you mean? What's to come?" I tried to press myself to my feet, but my body felt stuck to the wall.

"She is now one with Michael, his desires are hers. There will be less and less of her inside that body with every minute that passes, Vincent's plan was one that will appeal to him though." The old man seemed to be fuzzy around his edges now, blurring a little.

"Quickly something is happening, tell me what you know." I shouted.

"Yes they are pulling you back." He looked to his left as though viewing someone. "She will attack the castle with what small force she has, they will find every creature known on record and hunt them down to enslave them into an army, anyone who resists will be killed. Michael wanted the world as his own, humans will be turned or killed dependant on how useful they are deemed. Your mother's blood mixed with the vampires has a strange property, she is born of light magic at its very strongest. Vincent believed it would create a race of vampires who would be able to withstand the sun."

"They'll be able to go out in the day." I gasped.

The old man nodded fiercely. "I don't think it will work to the extent they believe but I would imagine it will allow them to be exposed to some diluted daylight. You must stop her." He reached for me his hands nothing but a blur. "The soul has to die within its vessel. If removed it will just bounce into another, it has been released from its sleep and the only way to end it is to kill whatever it is in at the time. Do not try to remove it Ruta, it will only pass to someone else and they may be weaker and much easily manipulated to do terrible things. Do you understand?" I nodded but the cave was spinning, the colours and shadows running into one another. I scrunched my eyes closed tucking my head against my knees as the world seemed to drop.

"RUTA!" Regina's voice was sharp and loud. "Sarro do something!" She screamed.

"She's back." Sarro's voice sounded exhausted, I felt her hand leave my arm. Lifting my head carefully I scanned my surroundings, I was in the cave, every person present was staring at me with varying levels of fear.

"Ruta?" Regina reached for my face and cupped my chin gently.

"I'm OK." I mumbled.

"What happened?" Hannah was at my side her hand grabbing my own.

I looked over at the body, his face still visible now looked somehow peaceful his eyes closed softly, I sighed and began to explain.

CHAPTER SEVENTEEN

It looked smaller than she remembered, this castle, this legendary place, this supposedly impenetrable fortress. Marina felt his confusion inside her mind. Was it so very long ago that she had been here? She closed her eyes as a memory pushed hard to be seen, two girls, smiling at a bedside. The presence within her fought back clawing up forcing her to open her eyes. She focused her gaze on the stone walls, noting the crumbling mortar holding them together, the long strands of ivy digging against the window frames. How had it withstood so much for so long and held so much power, this crumbling ancient building? She clicked her fingertips and four bristling wolves appeared, their coats black, stark and standing on end. She eyed them with disgust. "You know what to do." She said sternly. The wolves yapped and yammered eager to move, their jaws snapping at one and other in agitation, yellow eyes blazing. "So go." Marina said in almost a tone of boredom. They bounded forwards racing down the slope.

In an upper window of the castle, Henry Belladon watched the oncoming werewolves, he strained his eyes through the diamond crosses laced within the glass. Bard had been sure they would attack tonight even though there didn't seem to be many of them, the group of advanced students below shielding the main steps shifted nervously, their hands clutched tightly around shining silver edged weapons. In the tree tops Henry could just make out the shapes of the most experienced hunters, the first line of defence waiting to pounce. His heart hammered against his rib cage, bile rising into his throat as he swallowed down his fear, the four lean shapes were streaking through the gaps in the tree's, moonlight catching them causing a ripple of light on their fur. Henry looked back towards the rocky outcrop where a woman stood statuesque, too far to see her features clearly but the ebony hair and staring emerald eyes were enough. Marina, he shook his head sadly.

"Is that her?" Mia was at his side, her hands pale on the glass of the window.

"I believe so." Henry nodded sadly.

"Yeah it's her." Greta agreed glaring into the night. "I can feel her."

"Are all of the students safely underground?" Henry turned to a guard who was stationed at the now barred doors of the top tower, the man nodded briskly. "I still think you two should have gone down there too." He mumbled turning back to the girls.

"No I couldn't be down there not knowing what is happening, my whole family is out there." Mia shook her head fiercely.

"And anyway, we're at the top of a castle, surrounded by guards the doors are barred with silver and iron, the stairs have been coated with liquid silver, there is no way for anyone to climb up here all the ivy has been cut down. We are literally unreachable." Greta shrugged.

"I don't know about that so much." Henry muttered turning back to the window frame. "We need to stay as quiet as possible and remember stay out of sight. If they see you up here Mia they won't give up trying to reach you."

Mia nodded but remained silent inching back a little into the shadows. A blood curdling howl ripped through the night, it began as a bark before morphing into a scream. A man tumbled through the last of the trees falling to his knees on the open grass, he clutched at a hole in his stomach where inky black liquid was pumping freely from between his ribs, his teeth bared in a snarl as he sank to the ground before falling still.

"Werewolf." Greta muttered. A series of growls erupted from either side of the driveway, two of the wolves stepped into the light their heads turned to take in the sight of their fallen comrade they edged towards the cluster of hunters lining the steps, snarling and snapping.

"Move back." Henry whispered placing his hand on Mia's arm.

There was a pause then an eruption of noise and movement as the hunters flew into action, the sound of metal connecting with flesh mingled with the yelps and gasps of the fallen werewolves.

"Reform." Bard shouted roughly, there was a shuffling and the line of soldiers stood solidly once more, the bodies of three men laid out before them.

"There's one still missing." Henry said scanning the trees.

"Maybe they got it in the woods." Mia shivered.

"Is it just me or has it just gotten really cold all of a sudden?" Greta asked her breath frosting on the air.

"No it definitely just got colder." Henry was shaking, beads of frost forming across his moustache as he spoke.

The men and women below dropped their weapons as the metal froze and bit into the flesh of their hands, recoiling as though burnt they looked to one and other with confusion.

"To the left!" Bard shouted. Mia strained her eyes over the window ledge, her fingertips stinging as she gripped the stone. Her mother stepped into the open space silently, the one remaining wolf bristling at her side. The hunters scrabbled to pick up the weapons, Marina lifted her hands a cruel glint in her eyes and a smile playing on her lips as the people before her crumpled to the ground clutching at their throats.

"Witch!" Bard screamed, he slammed his hands into the wheels of his chair but they were frozen solid refusing to move. Marina tilted her head towards him and clenched her fists tightly, a crack of bones rang out in unison and every soul fell flat and still.

"Hello Mr Bard." Marina's voice sounded strange, not quite her own.

"You will pay for this." Bard spat. "Coward!"

"Oh no, not cowardly, clever." Marina gave a short laugh and pressed her hair casually behind her ear. "Why waste time and energy when it can just be over so quickly." She clicked her fingers. "Snap, like that."

"Using magic to defeat an enemy that makes you a coward." Bard hissed.

"Using children to protect yourself that makes you a coward." Marina countered.

"I need to do something." Mia whined. "Maybe she would listen to me."

"No." Henry gripped her hand firmly. "She isn't herself she won't listen to anyone."

The man in the wheelchair ground his teeth, his hands shaking with anger hovering above the wheels. "So what now?" He asked.

"Well, I have to kill you." Marina placed her hands on the arm rests of the chair and leant in seductively. "But I will give you a chance to change that." Bard shot his hands up wrapping them around her throat. He grinned squeezing tightly.

"Is that it? That was your move?" Marina laughed completely untouched, slowly his hands peeled away from her as though prised apart by an invisible force, Bard gasped and pushed back but it was futile he let his arms fall limp at his sides. "Now that we have gotten that out of the way, where are my daughters?" Marina stood up and placed her hands on her hips.

"You really think they would want to be anywhere near you?" Bard gave a harsh laugh.

"I am their mother. Of course they want to be with me." Marina smiled tightly but her top lip curled into a snarl.

"Well then, you are crazy." Bard said calmly.

"Where are they!?" Marina screamed making Mia jump stifling a squeak with her hand.

"Gone." Bard laughed.

"Gone?" Marina questioned her cool façade returned. "Well they can't simply disappear so you must be either lying or you know where they have gone to. No doubt that sister of mine has something to do with it."

"They have gone, to hunt you down." Bard smiled broadly. "After all you aren't really their mother anymore are you? You're a monster."

"You always were observant." Marina grinned.

"The blackness inside you, it isn't even controlling you against your will. You have given it free rein, like you always did, easily controlled, pliable!" Bard laughed.

"Oh Bard." Henry ground his teeth. "Stop talking."

"What does he mean?" Mia whispered. "What is in her?"

"Something bad, I can see it shimmering off her like a cloud, it's like she has two shadows one just on top of the other." Greta shuddered.

Marina smiled softly. "It's ok." She reached forwards and pressed her hands either side of Bard's head using her thumbs to hook against his eyelids forcing them wide, they both fell still.

"Thank you." Marina stumbled back a step, her breath hitching in her throat.

"You coward!" Bard shouted spit flying from his shaking lips. "That's the only way you can get what you want, by magic and trickery you have no honour no real talent or bravery."

"I have all I need to know." She turned her back and nodded to the wolf who sprang forward, cutting off the man's scream before it even had a chance to pass his lips. Mia gasped as the wolf tore into his neck toppling the chair over. Greta reached forwards slamming a hand over her lips.

"Oh Mia." Marina's voice called softly, a rustling of branches indicated the presence of the rest of the vampires who had been lurking out of sight. "In the basement." Marina said loudly. "Go through them all until you find my daughter, kill any who resist."

"No!" Mia shot to her feet banging her hands on the glass as Henry pulled at her waist. Marina's eyes flew to the window.

"Wait!" She shouted to the vampires who stopped sullenly. "Mia be a good girl and come down here so that I don't have to kill all of those lovely children."

"Mia you can't!" Greta growled.

"I have to." Mia straightened up her dress shrugging off Henry's hand. "I have to." She repeated solidly. Greta shook her head feverishly.

"I won't let you." She cried.

"Find Ruta and tell her what's happened. She will find me, she will fix this." Mia's bottom lip wobbled, she turned to the guard at the door. "Open it please." He looked at Henry who was gawping dumbstruck. "Open the door!" Mia sobbed. He quickly lifted the bar and carefully nudged open the door allowing her to pass through. Mia stepped down the spiralling staircase her shoes slipping on the rivets of molten metal that had dried to form a shining river.

"There you are." Marina was waiting at the foot of the stairs.

"Mother, why are you doing this?" Mia cried as she moved into the open shadowed by Marina.

"I have to darling." Marina sounded almost pained for a moment. "Don't you see we have been held back for so long? The world needs a reminder of what true power looks like. Don't be afraid, you will be a princess." She leant forward and smoothed her hand over Mia's dark hair.

"Start with those two." Marina indicated over her shoulder towards the tower where Greta shrank back from the window.

"No! I have done as you asked, I am here." Mia jumped into the doorway throwing her arms out into the gap.

"Ok if it means that much to you." Marina shrugged. "Let's get inside and start taking the logs and registers of activity, anyone who won't help or tries to get in the way, kill them. Any of the adults who are strong and fit enough bring to me, I will turn them myself we need to replace the ones that are lost."

"Mother!" Mia cried.

"You know, ideally I wanted your sister." Marina bit her bottom lip as Mia stared in disbelief. "But you will do, you have my blood after all but not quite my fire, who knows maybe that will change." From inside the castle a chorus of screams began rising. "This will only hurt for a minute." Marina smiled and before Mia had a chance to react, she punched a needle into the centre of her chest puncturing the black fabric of the dress and pushed down the plunger.

Greta screamed from the top window of the tower, her feet kicking as Henry desperately tried to wrestle her to the floor. Mia fell onto her back, her heart beat loud in her ears slowing as a blanket of cold crept over her limbs. "Welcome to your new family." Marina smiled and placed a kiss gently on her daughters head before turning and walking away.

CHAPTER EIGHTEEN

Regina kicked her horse forwards, the smell of the blood had reached her over half a mile away and without a word she had left the group and rode hard, vaguely aware of Hannah shouting her name as she tried to keep up. She signalled the mare to stop and jumped off, her feet crunching against the gravel. A trail of fluttering papers stretched across the grounds, sheets of white stark against the dark grass, bodies lay scattered down the wide stone steps. Regina pulled a knife from the folds of her dress and edged closer, giant imprints of splayed paws and the stench of the wolves made her wrinkle her nose in disgust, she moved past Bard stepping silently over his upturned chair avoiding the pool of blood and slipped inside the hall. Long slicks of crimson patterned the wooden floor, bodies of the documentarians had been hauled into corners bitten and mauled then left to line the walls. Regina lifted her face sniffing the air before moving into a corridor to her right where candle stumps guttered in the walls. A fingertip stretched out and touched her ankle making her leap back with a hiss. A man, he tried to speak, a trickle of blood slipping down his chin.
"Who did this?" Regina squatted before him the knife still clutched in her hand.
"She was a demon." He spluttered.
"She?" Regina's voice quivered.
"Yes, she laughed as they tore them apart." He cried a gurgling guttural sob.
"They? Who is they?" Regina clutched at his shoulders but his eyes rolled upwards and he slumped down against the flagstones.
"Regina!?" Hannah shouted through the open doors, the blue beam of the sight on her gun darting through the darkness.

"I'm in here." Regina called back. Hannah edged around the door gun held out before her.

"It's ok there isn't anybody here. They have gone." Regina slid into a sitting position the knife resting against her palm.

"What the hell happened?" Hannah clicked a torch on and shone it around illuminating the carnage. "Is anyone alive?"

"It was Marina. She must have a following with her of at least a dozen vampires and werewolves judging by this." Regina sighed.

"Marina? Did this?" Hannah stared in disbelief.

"I can smell her, but it's different, there's something else to her scent." She shook her head. "Maybe it's the vampire in her."

"Did anyone survive? Where are the students?" Hannah moved closer avoiding the body of the man.

"The children!" Regina leapt up and sprinted down the hallway.

"I hate the way you do that!" Hannah huffed as she followed trying to keep up.

"The basement. If they had any kind of warning, which it seems they did by the small array of hunters outside the doors, Henry would have sent them down here." Regina skipped down the wide stone steps taking them two at a time before stopping outside a solid silver door. She pressed her fingertip against the mouth of a stone gargoyle that held a candle up against the wall and leant forwards.

"It is safe, open the door." She said loudly. A moment later a faint buzzing noise sounded accompanied by a voice.

"How do we know that you aren't one of them?" A man asked.

"I am Regina Ottoman, I have been a friend to this castle for a very long time. I can touch this door, I am no vampire." She placed her hands against the metal. "Your sister was a friend to this place once too." The voice, she realised was Dr Vause.

"My sister is no longer herself." Regina sighed. It fell silent for a moment, then with a loud series of clicks the door swung inwards.

"It is good to see you Regina." Dr Vause smiled sadly. "Where is the rest of your party?"

"Following." Regina nodded and moved into the room where dozens of pairs of eyes fixed on her fearfully. "Where is Mia?" She scanned the gathered children.

"She and Greta stayed with Henry above ground, they were in the tower." Dr Vause said quietly. "He tried to get them down here, but they wouldn't come and there wasn't enough time to argue."

"Do not bring the younger children out of here yet, anyone you think may be able to handle it should start cleaning up the mess upstairs." Regina looked at him meaningfully.

"Is there a lot to do?" Dr Vause rubbed at his temple sorrow coating his face.

"I am afraid so." Regina patted his shoulder and headed back up the stair well.

"Where are you going?" Hannah jogged to her side.

"To get Mia." Regina replied without breaking her stride.

"I'll come with you." Hannah grabbed for her hand and squeezed it. "It'll be ok, it will all get sorted out."

"I don't think this is something that can ever be fixed." Regina gently pulled her hand away. "But thank you for caring."

They broke into a jog and soon broke from the castle walls into the air, Regina glanced upwards at the tower.

"Why haven't they come down?" She asked.

"Maybe they're hiding and don't realise that it's ok." Hannah shrugged and moved towards the stairwell.

"No, they would have been watching." Regina shook her head, fear prickling her skin. She followed Hannah as they moved carefully upwards.

"Henry?" Hannah tapped the doors. "It's ok they have all gone you can open the doors now." From inside a grating noise sounded, the bar being lifted up and out of place, clunking heavily to the floor before the click of the locks and the doors inched open. Regina pushed her way through stopping and staring at Greta who was curled into a ball her head in her hands.

"Where's Mia?" She barked. Henry, who was also slumped against the wall stretched out his hand to the window sill and pulled himself to his feet shakily.

"Marina was here." He said almost apologetically. "We couldn't stop her."

"She took her?" Hannah gasped.

"Not exactly." Henry rubbed a hand over his hair.

"He let her go." Greta sobbed, lifting her face to show blood shot eyes and red cheeks.

"Explain." Regina spoke quietly but the menace in her voice was clear.

"Marina realised Mia was here, she threatened to start killing the children, she knew where they were. Mia wouldn't let her, she wouldn't let us stop her she exchanged herself for them." Henry swallowed hard.

"They could never have got into that basement Henry, you know that." Regina growled.

"I don't know what anyone is capable of anymore." Henry broke into tears. "Nothing is as it should be, everything good is turning bad everything strong is dying!"

"It's not his fault." Hannah said quietly.

"So where did she go?" Regina tried to keep her voice steady.

"Tell her!" Greta was hysterical her face shaking with rage.

"Tell me what?" Regina narrowed her eyes as Henry glanced nervously from side to side.

"I don't know how to." He admitted.

"Then I will." Greta wobbled to her feet and stood as straight as she could glaring at the old man before turning to face Regina. "She injected her." She said bluntly.

"What do you mean?" Hannah asked frowning.

"A syringe full of black blood, straight into her chest." Greta mimicked the action on the plunger being pressed.

"No!" Regina staggered back a step, what little colour she had draining quickly from her face.

"Yes. Mia is a vampire now too." Greta sobbed.

CHAPTER NINETEEN

Everything felt so cold, from the tips of her fingers to the very outer edges of her ears. Mia carefully opened her eyes, blinking away what felt like a layer of grit, she was staring straight up at ceiling made of compacted earth. A low humming came from the corner where a small generator vibrated with life, a string of fairy lights had been stuck in between exposed tree roots and rocks to loop around the walls.

"I found them in one of the rooms in the castle, I thought you might like them." Mia turned her head sharply, her mother was seated in the shadows her back to the door, a teddy bear in her hands she turned its body round and around slowly between her fingers. "This was yours once, when you were very small. Ruta always wanted it, but you wouldn't give it her." The woman smiled softly. "You shared all of your toys with her, everything apart from this." She pressed a fingertip to its black nose. Mia raised herself so she was sitting, scanning where she was.

"Is this a cave?" Mia croaked her voice cracking with dryness.

"Yes." Marina leant forwards and offered a cup. "This is where Vincent kept me hidden for all of those years. That was the bed he slept on." She nodded to the worn camp bed that Mia was occupying. Mia shifted slightly before taking the drink and gulping down the contents.

"Better?" Marina smiled.

"Yes." Mia nodded and placed the cup onto the ground.

"It is ironic isn't it?" Marina looked up at the ceiling. "I wanted to get out of this place so badly and now it's our sanctuary."

"I feel cold." Mia rubbed at her arms.

"You will for a little while, your heart stopped pumping the blood around your body but it's moving again now, slower than what you are used to but it will soon warm up." Marina crossed her arms over her knees.

"What did you do to me?" Mia placed a hand on her chest.

"I injected you with my blood." Marina explained. "It means that the vampire in you is more diluted than in me. You share your DNA equally between witch and human, my blood has added just a touch of the vampire gene and strengthened the witch." She frowned for a moment. "At least that is what I hope has happened."

"I'm a vampire?" Mia spluttered.

"No, don't be dramatic." Marina rolled her eyes. "You have only got some vampire blood, you aren't fully turned."

"Why would you do this? They are cruel and evil, they kill for fun, they are our enemies!" Mia broke into a sob.

"No, no, no. That is what we have been led to believe but it is all wrong. You see the idea that Baron had, it was the right one. Why should we, creatures of power and magic, be limited to live a life hidden away, deprived of pleasure and with our gifts and natural instincts restrained and suppressed?" Marina was talking excitedly. "We shouldn't! We are ruled by a race that don't deserve their position of power on this planet, they should be subservient to us!" She banged a fist into her chest. "But unlike Baron, I do not want to enslave humans, I want to wipe them out entirely."

"You want to kill everyone?" Mia gasped.

"No of course not! The ones who are useful will be turned, some will be kept as feeding stock. We can create a new race." Marina smiled broadly.

"Have you lost your mind?" Mia was crying freely.

"You will see, in time you will understand." Marina reached for a jug and filled up the empty cup once more. "Still thirsty?" Mia paused in wiping at her tears, her throat did feel dry and scratchy, her stomach painful as she moved. "I know you are." Marina stretched out her hand with the cup once more. "You see you are already carrying out your natural behaviour." She added as Mia gripped the cup and drained it once more. Nervously she wiped a hand across her mouth pulling it away to examine the liquid coating her lips, it was thick and red.

I had no idea where she had taken my sister but that didn't stop me from pacing the room telling everyone present that we should leave immediately and begin the search.

"Ruta we don't even know which way she went. It's like she vanished, there isn't a single track." Hannah said gently as I strode past her once more.

"Magic, she used magic." Seraph pulled long and hard at her cigarette, the red lipstick coating the end.

"I am well aware of that." I hissed.

"Now, now, there's no need for that attitude." Seraph flicked the ash casually onto the floor and I saw Henry physically twitch.

"There's every call for that attitude." I spat back.

"Not in this room or with this company." Seraph's voice raised and I flushed with embarrassment.

"I'm sorry." I mumbled and sank into an armchair.

"Quite alright." Seraph turned away from me. "Where is that niece of mine?"

"She went to lie down for a while, I can go and wake her though." Hannah offered eagerly.

"No that won't be necessary." Seraph smiled.

"So what do we do?" I grumbled.

"We wait." Seraph began to take the pins from her hair, letting it fall curl by curl onto her shoulders. "There is nothing we can do to reverse what Marina has done to Mia, but what we do know is that she came here looking for information and when she realises that what she wants isn't in her hands, she will return."

"So we just sit here and wait for her to attack us again, what so more people can die?" I could feel the anger bubbling up in me.

"No we wait for her to come and try to bargain with us." Seraph teased a stray pin from strands of hair and placed it with the others atop the table.

"Why would she bargain with us? Didn't you see what she did last time she came here? It won't be any different." I tried to keep my voice steady.

"That is where you are very wrong, it will be entirely different." Seraph shrugged her shoulders tossing her hair from side to side. "This time she will know we are here."

"A couple of witches and a few hunters, yeah that will frighten her!" I scoffed.

I had barely turned my head when Seraph appeared beside me, the rest of the room seemed frozen, Hannah was turned in her seat halfway between standing and sitting, Henry was swilling wine around his glass, it sloshed suspended up one side.

"I don't expect for one second that she will be concerned about them or you, but she will be terrified of me." Something dark passed across the older woman's face, her eyes flashed in the firelight as she leant in to where I was pressing myself backwards in my chair. "She knows me and she will not underestimate what I can do. Trust me when I tell you that we are far from beaten and she will know it. I intend to take out of her whatever is lodged inside and see if we can salvage some of her humanity, but if we cannot." Seraph ground her teeth as she fixed her eyes upon my own. "If we cannot, then you need to prepare yourself, as I have, because I will kill your mother before I see the evil parasite that is living in her walk freely into another."

"What about Mia?" I asked nervously.

"She will be a lot simpler to deal with. As far as we know, there isn't anything or anyone residing in her apart from her own soul and from all accounts she has always been a very sweet gentle girl." Seraph looked at me expectantly, I nodded in agreement. "So, she may be entirely able to control whatever, urges, this blood may have given her."

"But if she isn't able to control them?" I said quickly.

"We can cross that bridge when we come to it. For now I will trust my instincts that she will be ok." Seraph moved back to her seat and reached for a fresh cigarette, she sparked up the end and pulled on it puffing smoke upwards, Hannah stumbled forwards her hands landing with a thud against the wooden table. Henry sloshed the wine over himself.

"Why do I feel sick?" Hannah asked steadying herself as she swayed a little.

"Your jet lagged darling. It will pass in a moment." Seraph waved her hand nonchalantly.

"You froze us again didn't you?" Henry huffed reaching for his handkerchief and wiping at the puddle of red that was seeping into his trousers.

"Sorry." Seraph grinned. "We just needed a moment."

CHAPTER TWENTY

Tom kept low, his belly dragging along the ground, nose pointed forwards as he sniffed long and hard. They vampires hadn't left any tracks but they had been careless as they'd moved through the woods, fingers brushed against tree trunks left the scent of blood coating the bark. Tom crept forwards, moving silently under tree branches his ears twitching constantly back and forth, he gazed up at the wall of rock his teeth bared as he realised where Marina had gone. All those years Vincent had held her against her will and now this is where she returned, with a daughter she had sentenced to an existence of darkness. He snarled and moved back towards where Sarro was quietly crouched, skipping inside a thicket of brambles he stifled a yelp as he morphed back into human form.

"She's in there." Tom rolled his head back an inch as he buttoned up his trousers and shrugged on a thick woollen jacket. "I am certain of it."

"I guess it was the obvious place for her to go." Sarro sighed. "She only ever really had a few options, we were stupid not to think of this as one." The witch turned heel and loped along the path back towards the castle, Tom hopped into his shoes and quickly followed.

"She must be quite sure of her powers to go somewhere that we know." He puffed.

"She is. She always was. But now, with whatever else is in her blood, she will truly believe she is unstoppable." Sarro strode over a fallen branch. "Maybe she is." She muttered.

"Don't say that." Tom growled.

"Not saying it doesn't make it any less true." Sarro snapped picking up her pace and moving ahead.

"So what are we doing then? What is the point of any of this if it's hopeless?" Tom stopped and placed his hands on his hips watching Sarro disappear between the branches.

"She's gone back to the cave where Vincent had her hidden." Greta burst into the small bedroom where I was lying staring up at the ceiling. I sat bolt upright.

"Is Mia there with her?" I asked.

"I don't know, Sarro is on her way back she sent the message to me. She can't be far now, I have been looking everywhere for you!" Greta huffed moving back out of the doorway as I barrelled past her into the hall charging down the stairwell.

"Hannah!" I called as the woman darted into the dining room.

"Ruta, you've heard the news then?" She stepped towards me her blond ponytail swinging at the base of her neck as she moved.

"Yes. What's the plan?" I fell in step beside her as we pushed open the wooden doors.

"Well." Hannah stuttered, the room was bustling with people.

"Regina?" I caught hold of my Aunts hand as she darted past.

"Good you two are here. The armourer is over there, go see her." She pointed towards the corner where an old hunched woman was flicking through a piles of greaves and vambrace.

"Whoa hold on." Hannah held an arm out to stop Regina moving away. "Who are all these people and what do we need armour for?"

"They are witches mainly, Seraph still has a lot of pull within our race, when people heard what was happening and that we needed help, they came." Regina gave a proud smile.

"Ok and the armour? You do know we have bullet proof vests now right?" Hannah grunted as a small woman nudged her to one side.

"Bullet proof vests are not going to help against vampires." Seraph appeared, her eyes glinting as she watched the witches moving around the room.

"You look terrifying." I scanned my eyes up and down my great Aunt, she looked magnificent with solid silver breast plate and her hair scooped back from her face held in place with a shining emerald studded tiara.

"Thank you darling." She smiled and pressed a cigarette into the holder before raising it to her lips. Regina rolled her eyes and moved away.

"I guess I best go this way." Hannah patted me on the shoulder before disappearing.

"Do we really need all of this?" I tapped Seraph's metal coated wrists.

"Yes." She answered simply. I reddened and looked away.

"If one of those creatures tries to bite you, this could be what saves your life. Let him sink his teeth against solid silver, they would break to pieces." She blew smoke up into the air her lip curling with anger.

"It could be a 'her'." I muttered.

"Yes, it could be your quite right." Seraph nodded in agreement. "Go and see Sonja before all the good pieces are taken."

"Ok." I sighed and moved away towards the old woman, her fingers were gnarled and red as she wove cords between pieces of leather.

"Ah!" She looked up at me her eyes pink and watery. "I wondered when I would see you."

"You know me?" I frowned.

"There's no mistaking you. You are your mother's daughter." She chuckled and reached for a solid piece of silver.

"In looks maybe." I answered. Sonja rose shakily to her feet and began to press pieces of metal against me, tightening them into place as I stood awkwardly letting her dress me.

"No, it's more than your face." She added after a few moments. I took a deep breath, the weight of the armour making me shift uncomfortably.

"What do you mean?" I asked.

"Your heart is not unlike hers when she was your age." Sonja patted the chest piece proudly. "You're all done."

"I don't understand." I stayed standing as the older witch retook her seat.

"I can see the strength of people, the true colours of the heart. Your mother was always giving off the deepest red, but there were small parts that blended into dark. Hidden away, lurking in the corners but there none the less. You are the same." Sonja looked at me carefully, gauging my reaction.

"I think we all have that in us." I shrugged trying to brush off the nervous energy trembling through my fingertips.

"No, we don't." Sonja shook her head. "You're Aunt, Regina, she is the brightest red, with amber and orange at the very edges."

"Doesn't it ever change?" I couldn't keep the plea from my voice.

"Yes of course." Sonja nodded slowly. "It adjusts with the emotions at the time but the base colour, the foundation so to speak, that never changes it is always the same."

"But that would mean if there is good in your heart, then no matter what you do that it will always be there?" I questioned.

"Yes." Sonja agreed.

"So my mother, even though she has done bad things now, her heart will still have light in it?" I stared at the witch as she shook her head sadly.

"That is the only thing that damages a person beyond repair, killing someone else." Sonja looked up at me, her eyes full of tears. "It darkens the soul Ruta, there is no going back from that."

"What are you two chattering about?" Seraph appeared beside me.

"Nothing. I need to go." I bustled past my great Aunt and headed out of the room.

"Be careful what you tell her Sonja." Seraph spoke low but there was no hiding the warning in her voice.

"She asked the questions sister, I cannot lie to the girl." Sonja tilted her chin defiantly.

"You don't have to lie." Seraph leant in closer. "You just don't have to tell the whole truth. She doesn't need to know about all that, not yet, not while her gifts are still developing. There is enough to deal with at the moment don't you think?"

"You see it too don't you?" Sonja shook her head. "I should have known you could see it."

"Yes, I see it. But as far as I can tell, it hasn't come through her in any way shape or form as yet, even though she has been put through hell at such a young age. If she can control it now, in this environment, then maybe she doesn't need to focus on it at all." Seraph hissed.

"You're hoping it lies dormant." Sonja gave a laugh.

"It has so far!" Seraph growled.

"A lion, is still a lion even when it sleeps." Sonja's gaze turned to steel. "You can't deny the blood that is in her veins. She is her father's daughter as well as her mothers."

"She is an Ottoman!" Regina had suddenly materialised next to the two witches, her eyes blazed in the dim candle light.

"Yes she is. But she also has Murdoch's blood in her too." Sonja winced but held her eyes steady. "You know what he was, even if Marina wouldn't admit it."

"Enough!" Regina slammed her hands into the table sending sparks of red light shooting from the palms. The room fell silent as everyone turned to see what was happening.

"Ok Regina I think you are done here." Hannah tentatively placed a hand on the shaking arm of the witch and steered her away towards the doors.

"Are you pleased?" Seraph muttered.

"You need to be prepared to deal with whatever may surface Seraph. I have known you a very long time and all of your brethren with you, I have never seen a witch as young as her holding so much anger and power. It frightens me, it is merely simmering under the surface and if she doesn't know about it how is she supposed to recognise if it begins to try to take control?" Sonja whispered. "Her father derived from the Incubus race."

"I know what that man was!" Seraph spat. "He bewitched Marina, he stole her away all he wanted was her power to protect himself from all the enemies he had made. He never loved her."

"What's an Incubus?" I asked moving back into the room. Seraph span around to look at me. "What is it?" I repeated planting my feet solidly.

"Well, it looks like I have no choice but to talk to you about this now does it." She tightened her lips into a hard line snarling at Sonja before striding forwards and grabbing me by the arm pulling me out of the hall.

CHAPTER TWENTY ONE

It turned out the Incubi were a type of demon, one that preyed on people as they slept influencing their thoughts and feelings. A cruel race with no real capacity for love or genuine feelings, selfish and scheming.

"Well that makes sense, Matron Murdoch was vile." I sighed rubbing my hands through my hair.

"I'm sorry Ruta we should have spoken to you about it sooner." Regina sat opposite me on an identical metal framed bed, the medical unit was the only place I had been able to think of that was private enough for this type of conversation. Seraph paced the floor, her face flushed with anger.

"It was diluted down to almost nothing by the time it reached your father." She waved a hand. "I don't even know why we are discussing this."

"Diluted or not, it is still part of who I am." I said quietly.

"Your mother never believed it." Regina said. "She refused to see that what she was feeling wasn't real, there is no way she would have gone near him if she had been of her right mind."

"So what does this mean for me?" I looked up.

"The only thing that has shown through so far is that you can reach into another dimension of thought." Seraph said.

"That's it?" I looked from face to face.

"So far." Regina agreed.

"But that could change?" I groaned.

"It could but it won't." Hannah grabbed my hands and knelt in front of me. "I know you Ruta, you are good and selfless. You are going to be fine." I forced a smile.

"Yeah I will be fine." I tried to sound positive but my stomach churned painfully.

"We need to go. Every minute we waste here is another one that Mia could be suffering." Regina rose to her feet and held out a hand to me. "You are one of us Ruta, your heart is only pure. There will be time to talk about this when your sister is back with us." Her lip wavered as I grabbed her fingers and moved towards the stairwell.

The witches and hunters weren't the only ones preparing for a fight. In the cavernous hollow of the mountain Marina's soldiers were milling back and forth anxiously, more had joined their ranks, word of the upcoming battle had spread across the mountains into every crack and crevice rooting out the stragglers from Baron's force as well as new warriors. They snarled at one and other, barely engaging in any conversation, sizing each other up and sharpening stolen weapons. A few large wolves moved amongst them, teeth bared lips peeled back a mutual distrust clear between the creatures even though they were supposed to be fighting on the same side. Marina watched the group with mild interest, her seat crudely fashioned out of thick wooden pallets to form a throne of a kind that was raised up on a ledge a few feet above the ground. She trailed a hand over Mia's head as the girl sat at her feet trembling.

"Don't be afraid darling." Marina cooed. "Nobody here will ever hurt you." Mia flinched as the hand fell against the crown of her head once more.

"Or is it me you are afraid of?" Her mother halted in the stroking of her hair and instead tilted her chin towards her to examine her face.

"I don't know." Mia stuttered.

"Be strong now Mia, you are practically a princess here." Marina curled her lip in disgust at the weakness her daughter was showing. "Do not embarrass me." She released Mia's face with a rough shove.

"Don't push me like that!" Mia snarled jumping to her feet, her breath hitched in her throat and she shook as anger enveloped her body rushing into every vein.

"Yes! Get angry!" Marina stood also, smiling broadly, the vampires nearby edged back as Marina slammed her hands into Mia's chest sending her crashing to the floor. Mia screamed and leapt off all fours into the air lunging for the glowing green eyes of her mother who skipped to one side with a laugh.

"That's right, let all of that rage fuel your body." Marina jumped off the platform lightly and wove between the large bodies of the crowded men.

"I want to kill you!" Mia roared as she rushed forwards. "You should have stayed dead!" Her voice was hoarse but it echoed off the walls, returning to her ears making her freeze in her pursuit. "I don't recognise myself! That's not my voice." She sobbed raising her hands to her mouth. "I would never say anything like that." She scuttled back to the ledge scrambling up and balling herself against the chair.

"Oh! For a moment there I thought I was dealing with your sister." Marina pushed her way back through her army, tutting theatrically. "How disappointing."

"Stop it." Mia pushed her hands to her ears blocking out the sound.

"You really are the weakling, no use for anything. They should have left you in that car to die." Marina's voice sounded inside her mind making her snatch her hands away, her eyes homed in on her mother, the mocking smile and black ringed eyes. Her pulse drummed in her ears, slow but deafening she took a long breath and leapt, hands outstretched, fingertips clawing as they connected with flesh, tearing and ripping until blood ran across her skin. Mia realised she was still screaming, her hands hovered in the air, crimson droplets falling to the floor, soaking into her knees as they squeezed either side of the body she had slammed to the floor.

"Now that is more like it." Marina stepped into view clapping her hands slowly together. "Well done my love, well done." Mia looked down, a narrow man lay under her, his black eyes wide and staring, the bones of his throat and chest visible beneath the flow of blood that was streaming into the earth.

"What did you make me do?" She gagged and fell back onto her haunches scrambling to get away.

"Me?" Marina held a hand to her chest with mock incredulity. "I didn't do anything, this was all you." Mia sobbed and turned her head away, wiping her hands frantically against the dirt. "This is your nature now, embrace it." Marina smiled. "Dinner time boys." She called over her shoulder as the wolves loped from the shadows, saliva dripping in ribbons. "It is who we are."

"It's not who I am." Mia cried.

"Yes it is!" Marina raised her voice over the sickening crunches and snarls of the wolves. "You always wanted to be like Ruta, Ruta who gets to go everywhere and do everything!" Marina reached down and forced Mia to her feet to face her. "Why does she get to be the one who is always important? All those years you were held captive, do you really think that they didn't know about you?" Mia's eyes widened but her mother continued to lie. "They knew where you were Mia, they just didn't think you were worth the risk, they had Ruta to rely on to hope that she would grow to be the powerful witch that you were never expected to be. Think about it, Ruta gets to battle and fight, she gets to be trusted with secrets and information while you are brushed aside, kept occupied like a child." Mia felt her eyes burning as the anger wrapped around her heart like lead casing. "Even Tom, your Tom, he wants Ruta, he sees you like a child still even though you are a brave survivor just like her! In fact you are stronger! You spent years with vampires locked away, but here you are, still standing." Marina swept a finger over Mia's cheek. "You are the powerful one Mia, I just had to help you unlock it. You and I together, we are family my darling, we are equal." Mia's green eyes blazed as she blinked back tears, the pupils pulsing as a thick black line appeared to ring the emerald colouring. Marina smiled broadly.

"Tom and Ruta?" Mia growled.

"Yes my love they have been sneaking past you, thinking you are just a silly, weak child." Marina nodded. Mia's heart shuddered like a cloud had passed through it icy and wet, blackening the surface, she bared her teeth.

"I am not a child." She spat angrily.

"That's my girl!" Marina cooed turning away with a smug smile.

CHAPTER TWENTY TWO

Snow drops had begun peeking through the ground, their sleepy white heads dropping in patches all around the bases of trees. I held one gently between my fingers examining the translucent petals.

"Beautiful aren't they?" Tom said as he came towards me, hands tucked in his pockets, shoulders hunched making his mop of hair bunch out even further. I nodded silently and let go of the flower. "You nervous?" He sat himself down on the hard ground beside me and looked up at the castle.

"Yes." I admitted.

"That's good, I would be worried if you weren't." Tom grinned.

"This Incubus thing has messed with my head a little." I rubbed my knees as I brought them towards my chest.

"Yeah I can understand that." Tom looked at me carefully. "It's not about what's in your blood though that doesn't define who you are, you know that. I mean, look at me. I'm a wolf half the time! You know what the rest of my race are like, they kill and enjoy it too. I could have given in to that, the desire for blood, I know how it pulls at you and tries to take hold. But you can fight it."

"That's the thing though, I've never felt that way. I've never felt any kind of pull towards doing anything to hurt someone or to try to influence them in any way." I said eagerly.

"Well then what are you worried about?" Tom nudged me with a laugh. "Just because he was your father doesn't mean that you have that part of him within you."

"No, but what's the alternative? My mother." I sighed and leant my head against the backs of my hands.

"Hey." Tom reached forwards and with a gentle hand lifted my chin so that my eyes were on his own. "She wasn't ever bad. She was only good. This thing, whatever it is that has taken hold of her, it's using her like a puppet pulling the strings."

"Sonja, the witch armourer, she said she can see the colours of people's hearts, she said mine is like Marina's that we both have darkness in the corners of us." The words left a bitter taste in my mouth.

"Well I think we probably all have a bit of darkness in us." Tom scoffed.

"Apparently not." I muttered.

"Look Ruta, you are dwelling on something that you don't need to. You are good, your heart is good, amazing in fact." He stared at me with amber eyes. "You are the most incredible person I have ever met." Suddenly the feeling of his hand on my chin became noticeable, his fingertips exerted slight pressure as he tilted my face towards him before pressing his lips against mine. I froze as his mouth parted then resealed on my own, feeling his hair brush against my cheek as he moved a hand upwards cupping the back of my head.

"Tom." I flinched back scooting my body away an inch or so.

"I'm sorry, I just couldn't not kiss you." He blushed and dropped his hand to the floor. I stared forwards at the glittering windows, unsure what to do. "I'm sorry I obviously shouldn't have done that." Tom sounded annoyed.

"No it's fine, I just don't think...." I trailed off not knowing what I wanted to say, my heart drummed in my ears and confusion washed over me, did I want Tom to kiss me? Had I ever even thought of him like that? "My head is just all over the place, I don't know what I'm thinking or feeling right now." I finished lamely daring to glance at him, he caught my eye and nodded before hopping to his feet and stalking away. I watched him stride up the steps and disappear into the castle.

"Well played." The voice made me jump.

"Greta how long have you been there?" My face burned with heat as the young witch stepped out from behind a nearby tree.

"Oh long enough." She grinned and skipped towards me.

"Didn't you ever get told it's rude to eavesdrop?" I scolded.

"No." Greta smiled.

"No, of course not. In a family full of witches listening in is a 'gift'." I shook my head and stood up brushing strands of grass from the back of my cargo pants, the metal on my wrists clinked together.

"So, what are you going to do?" Greta reached for my arm and examined the silver casing. "About Tom I mean." She added.

"None of your business." I snatched my arm away. "And keep it to yourself please, I think we have enough to deal with right now." I moved towards the castle entrance and Greta fell in step beside me.

"Yes agreed. When do we leave?" She said eagerly.

"You are not coming." I pushed the solid door open wider and moved into the hallway.

"Yes I am!" Greta barked. "See if you can stop me!" Her eyes blazed.

"Ok talk to Regina about it, I'm too tired to argue with you." I rubbed at my eyes wincing as the heavy metal clunked against my cheek. "This armour!" I yelled.

"I don't think you should kiss her again." Greta turned her head and looked into the corner where a wolf was curled up on a thread bare rug, his yellow eyes glinting over the top of a bushy grey tail. "It makes her so grumpy!" She skipped out of reach as I tried to bat her with my hand.

"Greta shut up!" I muttered.

"It's supposed to make you happy, you're like a bear with a sore head, or a wolf with a sore...." Tom gave a low long growl cutting her off. "Ok, ok, nobody has any sense of humour around here." Greta huffed stomping up the stairwell. I glanced at Tom, he closed his yellow eyes immediately, I sighed and headed for the dining room.

We moved off from the castle before the sun came up, the clink of armour and thudding of hooves the only sound as we wound between the trees. Regina rode beside me silently, Hannah and Seraph a few steps behind us and Greta on foot skipping through the forest like a sprite. I allowed my head to roll back a little creaking at the neck, we had been riding for hours.

"There's a small village up ahead." Sarro called from the front of the line. Regina nodded. "It has been there for many years." She told me quietly. "They know of us and the castle, they know what we do and how we provide protection, there will be no problem passing through."

"I never knew anyone else lived out this far." I frowned.

"Yes, they make a living by providing the meals for the castle and cutting and selling timber. They fell it, then send it down river to the main town fifty miles away." Regina informed me.

"They make that mush?" I gawped. "I feel like stopping just to thank them."

"Sarcasm doesn't suit you darling." Seraph said from behind.

"You haven't had to eat the food!" I called back turning to look over my shoulder.

Sarro held up her hand halting her horse. A sharp buzzing rang in my ears making me dip my head, slowly Sarro's voice formed in my mind.

Ruta, tell Regina that I can sense death, the village is to our right I feel as though we must go there, do not speak loudly we do not need to panic everyone but something is very wrong here

The buzzing subsided and I turned to my aunt who was already staring at me expectantly, I relayed the message.

"Tell her to turn off the path at the mill, we will go into the town just a small party of us." Regina's mouth was tight and hard.

I reached out, throwing my thoughts towards Sarro who I could still feel pressing at the edge of my consciousness. She raised a thumb in acknowledgement and moved forwards.

"Regina?" Seraph questioned quietly.

"I will explain in a moment." Regina whispered.

We moved on once more, edging to the right where the trail split, a wooden building was being to appear, a huge wheel stationary at its side, the trees began to thin and stumps littered the forest floor. Regina held up her hand as Sarro did the same bringing the procession to a halt.

"Rest a few moments." Regina shouted looking around at the witches and hunters who began dismounting and dropping their packs and weapons to the floor. "Seraph, Hannah, Ruta." She looked at me for a second her eyes full of sadness. "Come with me."

We jumped down from our horses and walked towards Sarro who was waiting with her hands on her hips staring at the large water wheel.

"I can sense it too." Regina said briskly as Sarro began to speak.

"I don't think we need to go in there." Seraph was pale her hands seemed to be shaking. The three woman stood staring at the door to the ramshackle building, its wooden planks scarred and broken swinging on rusted hinges. I turned my attention back to the track that ran between through the forest, the river bubbled beside it.

"Are those houses?" I pointed to where several small triangular wooden huts were poking from the ground. "What's that on the floor?" Cold washed over me as I strained my eyes.

"Ruta, we don't need to go down there. We already know what has happened." Sarro placed a hand on my arm but I shrugged it off and walked ahead.

"Let her go." Regina's voice sounded further than it was. My feet felt heavy as I approached the small town, but I pressed myself onwards. The mound on the floor became clearer even as my eyes burned with the effort of fighting back tears. I fell to my knees. A small child, no older than five or six, lay crumpled in the dirt, her eyes wide and staring a milky film coating their surface. Blonde hair streaked with rusty red blood fanned out around her tiny face, scratches lined her throat and disappeared under the ripped woollen jumper. Circular puncture wounds marked her neck and wrists, even one of her bare ankles had been bitten. I picked up the woven leather shoe, fitting it in the palm of my hand its partner still clung to the girl's blueing foot. I leant forwards and tried to work the shoe gently back over her bare toes, touching her icy skin a tear fell from my cheek accompanied by a pain that ripped through my head sending me sprawling across the floor. Regina's voice calling my name echoed in my ears as darkness swallowed me.

"Hi." A small voice made me spin my head to the left, my eyes widened as the little girl who had just been lying dead at my feet, smiled at me sweetly, her feet swinging beneath her as they dangled from a tiny chair.

"How are you speaking to me?" I gasped.

"The same way the old man did." The little girl rotated a carved wooden duck between her hands.

"You're on another plane?" I asked trying to look around. "Why is it so dark here?"

"Oh it's not, it's just that you aren't allowed to see it 'til you're really, really here." She flicked her golden hair out of her eyes.

"Ok so you wanted to tell me something, that's why I'm here right?" I pushed myself into a sitting position.

"No silly." She giggled making me smile. "You asked me something, that's why you're here."

"I did?" I frowned.

"Yes you said 'who could do this'." She lifted her small hand and moved the duck through the air in a flying motion.

"I hate how this works!" I groaned.

"I think its super cool." She looked at me with big blue eyes and I fought back the urge to cry remembering the white orbs staring up blindly into the sky.

"So, who did this?" I gulped.

"I don't know which one it was, there were lots of them." Her small face wobbled with sadness. "It's hard to remember now, but first there were the doggies." She rumpled her nose. "They didn't look like our doggies though. Mummy started to shout but they knocked her over and then she was quiet." Her lip trembled momentarily, she glanced to the side and brightened. "But she's here now, with daddy and Hugo, so its ok." I looked off into the darkness but saw nothing.

"What happened next?" I said gently.

"A lady came, daddy said she was a witch but then she started biting people just like the vampires do so daddy said she must be a devil. All the vampires started breaking the doors and people were screaming, I hid under the table in the kitchen with Hugo until it got quiet again." She pulled at the hem of her jumper picking at a stray strand of wool.

"Why did you come out?" Tears were falling freely down my cheeks as she kicked her feet back and forth.

"I didn't want to but Hugo said we needed to find mummy." She bit her lip with two tiny pearl teeth. "We thought they had gone, but they were all just being fat and lazy."

"Fat and lazy?" I questioned.

"Yes." She nodded. "Like when you eat too much and you fall asleep. They were just lying around and all the people were still and quiet." Her eyes lowered and she examined the duck carefully. "The girl came then. We thought she would help us, she started talking to us asking our names and she was really nice even though her mouth was full of blood. But then they woke up and….." Her little voice trailed off.

"What did she look like?" My words caught in my throat.

"She had black hair and looked like you." She looked up at me with sudden mistrust. "Only her eyes were different, they had little black circles right around the outside." She wiggled her fingers in a circular motion.

"Marina." I hissed.

"No, that's not it, the witch woman shouted her name just before they got us. She said 'move Mia'." She puffed out her chest and raised her arm as she imitated the stern voice.

"Mia." I gasped raising my hand to my mouth.

"Yep!" She jumped down off the seat. "I have to go now, thanks for putting my shoe back on." She grinned and lifted her foot to show the leather sandal, then skipped away into the darkness. I took a sharp breath and closed my eyes tight as everything span around me, feeling the world come back into focus.

"Are you ok?" Regina was crouched in front of me, Seraph beside her with a hand atop my head. I looked at the body of the small girl now lying in Sarro's arms.

"We will bury her and the others." She said in reply to my questioning look. It was all I could do to nod before the tears took hold.

CHAPTER TWENTY THREE

Several of the witches held out the palms of their hands and muttered an incantation that lifted the mounds of soil from the ground and deposited it atop the line of bodies neatly wrapped in blankets. I tore my eyes away from the two smallest holes as the earth dropped in. Regina clutched my hand tightly, I gave her fingers a squeeze then turned and slowly made my way back towards the horses.

"It's a terrible gift to have." Seraph followed me, stopping next to Matisse and running her hand down his neck. "I mean, useful and wonderful, but heart breaking I'm sure." She reached into her pocket and pulled out the long cigarette holder, pushing it between her lips and lighting up.

"Her whole family were there." I felt weak still, my legs not quite solid beneath me. Seraph nodded and blew smoke into the air.

"Comforting to know." She gave a small smile, then without looking swiped at Matisse who was carefully trying to take the packet of cigarettes from her pocket with his teeth. "Never going to happen foaly." She glanced at him with a grin as he flattened his ears and turned his head away.

"I can't believe Mia could be part of this." I exhaled sharply.

"I don't think she would want to be Ruta, but what choice would she have? The fact that she tried to speak to the children and that they weren't afraid of her, it shows that she has not lost her humanity. She is still your sister." Seraph looked at me. "She isn't you Ruta, you may be twins but you are very different. She doesn't have your strength of character, she would be afraid to resist Marina and I fear, much more easily manipulated as well."

"What do you mean?" I asked.

"Marina isn't stupid Ruta, she knows what it takes to make people tick. It is obvious Mia has always felt inferior to you, flattery and undivided attention may prove to be the most powerful weapon your mother has at her disposal." Seraph flicked ash to the floor.

"Once I get to Mia, I know she will choose to come back with us." I stated.

"Do you?" Seraph lowered her voice as the rest of the group made their way back towards us. I didn't reply, but watched my great Aunt place her foot into the stirrup and jump gracefully into the saddle.

"We need to move." Regina said as she strode past me and grabbed a chunk of her horse's mane swinging upwards onto the mare's back.

I settled myself into the saddle, Conker hesitated then moved on after the others, his ears spinning back and forth in my direction, my stillness was confusing to him. I leant forwards and ran my hand down the crest of his red neck.

"It's ok, I just don't have any words right now, you follow the others I'm just going to be quiet for a while." I whispered. Conker swung his head around to face me and rested his muzzle softly against the toe of my boot. "Thanks buddy." I rubbed his head feeling the warmth beneath my hand.

We picked up the pace moving at a march through the forest, the trail becoming narrower, obscured by branches and fallen trees until we were forced to dismount and lead the horses. The group had stayed almost completely silent for the last three hours, the sight of an entire village slaughtered shocking everyone into a numb state of grief.

"We cannot get any further with the horses." Tom appeared through the underbrush hastily buttoning his trousers his wolf fangs still protruding over his lip.

"Why?" Hannah pulled her horse to a standstill and grasped a small pair of binoculars, focusing into the distance.

"It's too dangerous, most of the path is covered with fallen trees, the taller branches have snapped, I don't think there is enough cover to move all these people and animals through in one go. Anyone from above looking out will see the movement." Tom panted, he glanced at me quickly his cheeks flushing before turning away.

"Right well, there is only one thing we can do." Seraph jumped to the ground. "We can't leave them unprotected, we must make a camp for tonight and continue on foot in the morning."

"No we need to carry on now." Regina shook her head.

"My dear girl, take a look around you." Seraph spoke quietly. "These people are exhausted, we have been riding for hours we've buried children and seen horrific things. We haven't stopped to eat or stretch our legs. We have the fight of our lives when we get to Marina, we must be ready and at our very best." Regina looked around the group, it was true every single person was pale and exhausted, she sighed and nodded in defeat.

"Witches I need your help." Seraph clapped her hands.

"What do you need sister?" Sarro asked stepping forwards accompanied by at least ten others.

"This space between the trees." Seraph pointed to where the trees weren't so tightly knit. "We are going to get the hawthorn bushes to rise up and form a wall around the area to hold the horses, once that's done it needs to be enchanted so that none can pass through that are not of pure witch blood. That should keep away any unwanted visitors."

They nodded and moved into the tree line. I watched with amazement as under the barrage of muttered words and outstretched hands the spiky bushes grew and merged into a wall that spread outwards looping around tree trunks, the earth groaning under the stress of the searching web of roots. Greta was pulling bridles and saddles from the animals and sending each of them through the rapidly shrinking gap in the bushes where they cantered towards the centre shaking their necks loose.

"Is that all of them?" Seraph asked.

"Yep!" Greta smiled under armfuls of knotted rope.

"Seal." Seraph murmured holding out her hand. The hawthorn, not daring to resist shot into place closing over the space to form a solid barrier that stretched all the way around, at least five feet high. Two of the large hunter men, struggled forwards with a set of golden bales of hay, launching them with a grunt into the enclosure.

"They have the river running through for water." Seraph answered before I spoke. "The trees will provide cover from the worst of any weather, they will be more than fine."

We walked in silence towards where blankets had been rolled out across the smoothest parts of the ground, people were already lying flat atop them, eyes closed asleep or at least trying to be. The clicking and clunking of tins being opened was the only other sound as food was shared around.

"Hey." Hannah smiled at me and threw a can of chicken and rice in my direction.

"Thanks." I grimaced and pulled back the lid tipping some of the contents into my mouth.

"You're welcome." Hannah signalled us to come and sit with her. "How are you doing?" She swung her arm around my shoulder.

"I'm ok." I lied.

"I don't know what we're going to find in there Ruta." Hannah looked up towards the sky where the very top of the mountains peeked above the trees.

"I know." I placed the half empty can on the floor, nausea washing over me.

"I can't imagine what Mia must have gone through to be part of that back there." Hannah flicked her eyes towards the trail.

"I'm going to try and sleep." I said quickly getting to my feet.

"Oh ok." Hannah stood with me and reached forwards bringing me into a crushing hug. I patted her shoulder and turned away.

I felt as though I had barely closed my eyes when a tap on my leg woke me.

"Time to go." Regina whispered. I rubbed at my eyes, a fine mist was snaking through the air, clinging to the horse's manes in droplets as they watched us wide eyed. I pressed my hands to my hair, unwinding the elastic band so it tumbled loose around my face before scooping it back neatly and retying it in place. I got to my feet and gratefully accepted a hunk of bread from a tray that Greta was carrying between people.

"Did you get any sleep?" She asked.

"I think so, but I don't feel as though I did." I chewed the crust.

"Marina was searching last night, it took all my energy to keep my mind hidden, but I think she sensed me before I closed it off." Greta looked pale and beyond tired. "She didn't see anything apart from the sky, I was looking up at the time luckily."

"Did you tell Regina?" I struggled to swallow.

"Yes." Greta nodded. "She decided I should go back to the castle, it's not safe for me to be with you all. If we had been near the village or on the trail she might have guessed where we were."

"What about Sarro did she get into her head?" Anxiety was flooding every vein in my body.

"No." Greta pouted sullenly. "She has barriers around her mind that protect it, I've been trying to learn how to do it but it takes years and years."

"You'll get there Greta, you are one of the most talented people I have ever met." I rested my hand on her head. "But Regina is right we need to keep as hidden as possible and you need to be safe and waiting for when Mia gets back." At the mention of my sister's name the young witch almost crumbled on the spot, the tray wavering in her hands.

"If she comes back!" She hiccupped back a sob.

"Of course she's coming back!" I laughed. "Now go on, get out of here."

Greta looked at me through tear filled eyes. "Bring her back Ruta, no matter what it takes." She pleaded.

"I will." I nodded solidly. "No matter what."

CHAPTER TWENTY FOUR

Mia watched the vampires forming into lines, jostling and shoving each other with snarls and sharp words, she shuddered as they hoisted maces and swords, or tapped heavy wooden batons against the palms of their filthy hands. Marina observed it all with mild interest from her makeshift throne, her eyes ringed with ebony. An hour had passed since she had awoken the army, barking orders excitedly as everyone rushed to take their places.

"They aren't far away now. Can you feel it?" Marina grinned but didn't look at Mia who was silent with fear. "No of course you can't, you don't have as much power as me do you?" Marina rolled her neck loosening her shoulders.

"It doesn't have to be like this mother." Mia whispered, flinching as the woman span in her seat to face her.

"Is this how you want to be? This is how you want them to see you when they come through that wall trying to kill us?" Marina spat.

"They don't want to kill us." Mia's voice wavered under her mother's glare.

"Mia, they are coming with an army, however small and pathetic it may be it is an army none the less. Carrying weapons to use against us! Why else would they be here like this if all they wanted to do was talk?" She slid from her seat to kneel in the dirt. "They don't want us as family now Mia, we are no use to them anymore being what we are."

"That's not true, Ruta would never feel that way." Mia tried to sound certain but it was clear that doubt laced her words.

"If all they wanted was to ask us to come back to the castle with them, surely Ruta and Regina would have come alone? They know we would never want to hurt them, why should they be afraid?" Marina held her eyes steady even though the lie of what she was saying was burning through every vein. Mia shook her head but a frown creased her brow.

The voice inside Marina's head was gloating now, laughing urging her onwards subduing the part that shouted for it to stop, to cause no more pain to her child. The man, who she now knew as Michael, hushed her with a growl, his power beating in her chest making her fingertips tingle with the urge to fight. Mia watched her as she gathered herself sucking in a deep breath.

"We cannot go back now Mia, we are something different than them, they will never join us or understand what we need to do." She tried to sound sincere, knowing that the hope in her family's hearts would press them to try to save what was left of the soul in her body, that they would accept both Mia and herself back with open arms despite what they were, fools, the voice laughed. She pressed on. "We are all we have now, you and I." She reached out and cupped her daughter's clammy hand in her own. "You know that I am telling you the truth."

"My queen." A broad man stood before them, dressed in black faded denim jeans and bare chested, showing the tangle of dark veins that swirled over his heart and raced up his neck. He bowed briefly, tipping his bald head forwards. "They are through the tree line."

Marina smiled and waved her hand dismissively. "You can join me up on the outer ledge, you will see that I mean them no harm, we will give them the choice" She held out a hand to Mia pulling her to her feet and guiding her up a narrow walkway towards the hole that surrounded the trunk of the upturned tree.

The air hit Mia's face with an icy gust making her draw in a sharp breath, her eyes darted over the landscape coming to rest on the group of people who were milling at the base of the steep incline some forty feet below. She spotted Ruta and fought back the urge to call out, noting the heavy crossbow slung over her back and knives sheathed at her waist.

"Regina." Marina called down, her voice bouncing back around the open space. Mia watched Tom crouch low his clothes ripping to tatters as he broke into wolf form, snarling menacingly at her mother.

"Come down sister, let us talk." Regina held her hands outwards as Seraph quickly hushed the rising voices of the witches who spat out their disgust.

"Aunt Seraph? No it can't be, you don't look a day over sixty five." Marina smiled sweetly but Mia felt the grip on her hand tighten, the pulse in Marina's chest quickening.

"It's awfully rude of you to try and have a conversation from up there Marina." Seraph placed her hands on her hips and stared hard at her niece. "Surely you aren't too afraid to step amongst family." She reached into a pocket and pressed the cigarette holder into her mouth adding a cigarette and lighting the tip with a click of her fingers.

"That is a terrible habit." Marina tutted. "Rude as it may be I am thinking of my daughter's safety, it seems that many of you no longer think of us very kindly." She pouted and gazed over the gathered witches who all glared silently.

"You are wrong." Regina lowered her hands. "They have no issue with Mia, it is you they no longer recognise sister. How could you inflict this curse upon a child, your own child too?"

Marina turned to Mia and quietly muttered. "I told you Mia, they want me dead. There is no return for me and I had no choice in being this way, I admit it was selfish of me to do this to you but I didn't want to be alone again and I knew I would only ever be an outcast now." The voice inside her was screaming for blood.

Marina glanced into the tree line stretching her mind sharply to send a signal to a crouched vampire who lay hidden amongst the branches directly behind the witches.

"She's sending some kind of message." Sarro said quickly. "I can feel it but I can't understand its meaning." A whistle pierced the air making Regina duck as an arrow whipped through the sky racing towards the open ledge.

I heard the thud before I registered what had happened, my pulse slammed through my ears as I watched my sister topple forwards her knees crashing into the ground, the long wooden shaft of the arrow protruding from her chest. Regina raced forwards, her hands trying to desperately find purchase against the earth, her mouth was moving and I knew she must be screaming but I was enveloped in silence, my eyes locked onto the crumpled figure atop the rocks. Marina was bent over, her hands desperately pressing into the leaking black blood her face creased with agony she glared down at me.

"You shot her!" She screamed. Noise rushed back at me, the arguing voices of women from behind, the sob of my mother, a low keening howl as Tom crouched against the ground his ears flat to his head. I span around.

"Who fired that arrow?" My voice was calm and soft but everyone looked at me. "Not one of us." An older witch said defensively, I honed in on the bow in her hands, rage welling inside me until my flesh felt as though it was burning against my bones.

"You shot my sister?" I questioned stepping forwards.

"No I told you none of us fired a weapon, it came from behind." The witch was stumbling backwards.

"Ruta." Sarro grabbed my wrist, I threw her off slamming her to the floor with only the smallest of movements.

"You think you can shoot at MY sister!" I screamed.

"Stop this." Seraph appeared in front of me her hand held out glowing in the palm, I looked at her in disbelief.

"She just shot an arrow at my sister." I was shaking from head to toe.

"No she didn't. It wasn't one of us." Seraph took a step back as I moved forwards. "Don't make me do this Ruta." She warned.

"Get out of my way." I hissed, my own hands were flexing into balls, each time my fingers closed a red light glowed between them, Seraph noticed and her eyes widened with surprise.

"I can't stop you Ruta if you choose to do this that much is clear." She looked at my hands again then back to my eyes. "I didn't realise how powerful you are. But you don't need to do this, she did not shoot Mia." Seraph held her hands up but stood solidly in my way.

"Ruta, listen." Sarro had pressed herself to her feet and was beside me but stayed warily out of arms reach.

"I don't want to listen." I screamed, turning back around to look up at the ledge, Mia and my mother had vanished from view, I ground my teeth angrily.

"No you don't understand!" Sarro raised her voice. "I mean listen!" She shouted. "I told you seconds before that arrow was shot that Marina was sending a message but I couldn't read it, her mind is still open."

Seraph stared upwards. "It's not clear but I can hear it." Sarro pleaded. "Listen Ruta."

Regina moved back towards me her eyes blazing filled with tears. "Tom, go and check the tree line for any sign of enemies." Tom cocked his head but loped off all the same, his tail tucked between his legs.

"You." Regina pointed her finger at me. "Use this power you have and find out what the hell Marina is thinking." She grabbed the front of my jacket pulling me towards her.

"I can't hear anything." I growled shoving her off.

"Well try harder." She pushed me back and the light from my hands shot sparks into the earth.

"Regina." Hannah cried in warning, I looked over at her, she was afraid.

"Why are you scared of me?" I said incredulously, nobody answered.

"Ruta you need to find her mind. It's only you that is strong enough to do it." Seraph said quietly. I turned to Sarro she tilted her chin and eyed me back.

"What do I do?" I asked trying to calm my heart.

"Take a breath and reach out for her, think only of her, ask the question, seek her out. Her thoughts will be erratic, they will seem like a muddle of anger, maybe even colours I would imagine red's and blacks." Sarro nodded. "Try now before she gathers herself." I took a deep breath and turned to face the wall of rock, closing my eyes tightly I pressed my thoughts outwards.

CHAPTER TWENTY FIVE

Mia drew in sharp breaths. This felt different from when she had been shot, it was slower, colder there was more darkness no rushes of adrenaline pressing at her to keep on breathing. It was like verging on nothingness.

"It was supposed to hit me!" Marina screamed. "Where is he?"

"He has vanished my queen." The broad vampire was back, his hands knotted in front of him.

"Bring her blood!" She commanded. "How is this possible? I thought vampires couldn't die this easily?" She snatched the cup of crimson liquid from the outstretched hand and tipped it gently against Mia's lips. "Drink this my darling." She stroked the girl's bottom lip as she poured the blood into Mia's open mouth.

"It is easier than you would expect." The vampire replied. "If the heart is pierced or the injury is bad enough that the bleeding won't stop." He shrugged. "It is harder to kill us, but not even close to impossible." Marina groaned and threw the cup against the wall. "Her heart is pierced by the arrow, if you remove it she will only bleed out quicker, you cannot give her enough blood to equal the loss." He continued.

"Quiet." Marina held up a hand her eyes narrowing. "Impossible." She muttered as she felt Ruta's mind flittering through her thoughts, she focused and brought down the wall quickly. A moment of quiet, then Ruta screamed back into her head, she slid onto her haunches panic coating her face as she reached for the defences that would keep her thoughts safe. "How is she doing this!?" Marina gritted her teeth and pushed as hard as possible against the intrusion feeling it flood away to be replaced by the iron barrier she had long ago perfected. She breathed heavily sweat coating her face, if Ruta had seen what she had done, there was about to be a real fight.

"It was her!" I opened my eyes, stumbling with the effort. Tom reappeared, he snapped and snarled towards the trees baring his teeth then swinging around to howl towards the opening in the wall of rock.
"What did you see?" Seraph asked, quickly silencing Regina and Sarro.
"She had a vampire waiting to shoot, she wanted Mia to think it was us, it was meant to hit her." Ruta sighed.
"She did this!" Regina was shaking with anger.
"It was meant to hit her." I swayed again. "It was like pushing through mud to get to her. The way she threw me out of her mind, she's so strong." Hannah placed her hand on my elbow and pulled me to sit on the ground beside her. "Here." She handed me a piece of black sparkling sugar that had been pressed into squares. "Eat that."
"So what now?" I asked as I popped the cube into my mouth feeling it dissolve sweetly.
"We can't go in through that opening." Seraph was scanning the rock face.
"We don't have enough people and they will be waiting, it would be a turkey shoot. She knows you were in her thoughts, for her to fight you the way she did, she's afraid and that means she will be acting even more unpredictably"
"We know she has a fair amount of vampires with her from the attack at the castle and she gathered more at the village she ransacked." Hannah nodded in agreement. "If we go through there now they will just pick us off, it's too narrow."
"We need to find another way." Regina beckoned forwards two white haired young witches, they were lean like whippets, long pale legs protruding from below cotton shorts that had been patched and sewn countless times judging by the state of them. "This is Eros and Arya, they are our runners, our very best scouts."
"I remember your mother." Seraph nodded at them in acknowledgement. "She too was gifted with the speed of her feet."
"She was." Eros spoke quietly. "She taught us all that she knew, if there is another way into here we will find it."

"I have no doubt." Seraph smiled softly. "Go safely and be fast." The two women nodded sharply instantly turning and bounding away.

"What do we do?" I asked, my head boomed with a slow deep pain.

"There is nothing we can do until we find another way to attack." Seraph sat herself down beside me.

"Maybe we can distract them for a while, give the runners a chance to scout out the place without anyone seeing them?" I looked up at the dark hole. "Is it me or is that tree shaking?" I asked watching as the huge upturned tree that formed a bridge to Marina's hideout quivered. Seraph leapt to her feet.

"Move back! Everyone back to the tree line." She shouted. I scrabbled to my feet and lumbered forwards. A rumbling shook the ground and the sound of earth tumbling and falling echoed through the air, I glanced over my shoulder my feet snagging the ground as I twisted. The tree trunk hovered loose of all moorings, it twitched up and down pieces of stone and hard earth jumping from the creases in the bark. Then it flew. Soaring through the air, rolling slightly as it moved closer. I heard Regina scream my name but the pounding of my heart in my ears drowned her out, my hands clenched into fists and I willed my feet to move, but it was as though they had sprouted roots of their own and anchored me to the ground. I watched the huge log descending its shadow coating my entire body which burned with an all too familiar red anger, raising my hands above me Mia's smile flashed through my mind and a scream of my own erupted from between my lips. A burst of red light blinded me and I felt air rush past so fiercely it almost knocked me off my feet, the tree trunk exploded into tiny fragments and clouds of dust that billowed all around me obscuring the mountain from my view. I coughed and lowered my hands to my mouth stumbling away from the orange tinted air and jogging towards the tree line.

"Are you ok?" Hannah gawped at me and knocked dust from my jacket with her hands. I blinked trying to free my eyes from the grit.

"Here." Regina tilted my head back and poured water from a canteen over my face.

"I'm fine. I don't know what happened I just couldn't move." I rinsed my mouth with the water spitting out tiny pieces of bark.

"Your powers have definitely shown themselves." Seraph spoke quietly, eyeing me warily.

"I just held out my hands I don't know what happened." I said defensively, something about Seraph's expression made me feel embarrassed.

"Your magic took hold of you." She replied quickly. "You allowed it to control you, you let it feed off your emotions and it became a being of its own that you no longer had any say over."

"But you all do that at times, that's how magic works isn't it? It is in your blood it's just there naturally?" I looked at Regina who was frowning at me with almost sadness in her eyes.

"No." Seraph shook her head. "Magic is in our blood yes, but we have to work to reach it, we hone in our skills to use them we consciously decide when to apply a spell. What you just did, it isn't a good thing Ruta. You let something inside you take over and it used your magic without permission."

"So what you think I have something in me like her?" I was shouting pointing over my shoulder to where my mother was hidden away.

"No, you have your ancestors inside you Ruta." Seraph remained calm. "The incubi. They are a cruel race Ruta, do not let that part of you take over because you are in pain it will use your magic against your will and you may well end up lost to it."

"I defended myself!" I said in disbelief.

"Yes you did, but that red light, what if you were angry at one of us and it took over and you couldn't move or control it?" Seraph pleaded for me to understand. I looked around, those who weren't looking at me were staring at the floor nervously, those who were turned away quickly.

"You think I'm dangerous." The statement left me breathless.

"No Ruta." Regina came forwards and took my hand. "What your father was isn't your fault, but you cannot allow his genetics to take hold or use your magic, you are one of us, an Ottoman." She stroked my face with her hand. "When you feel that part of you rising in anger, you have to push it down, control it."

There were no words, I fell silent digesting what had just happened. I knew they were right to be concerned, I hadn't controlled any of what had happened I was merely a passenger. The knowledge that I had inherited my father's blood was like ice through my veins, however small a part I didn't want it.

"Come on." Hannah signalled for me to come and sit with her.

"It's ok. You can learn to shut it off, I know you can." She nudged me with her elbow as we watched the rest of the group arranging weapons and supplies a few feet away. I nodded swallowing down the urge to cry.

"Ruta, I have just managed to make contact of a kind with Mia." Sarro stepped towards me. "She is alive, but barely so." I gulped and examined my hands as tears stung my eyes. "I couldn't speak to her, her mind is almost empty like she is in a deep sleep, but I could feel her so I know she is still with us."

"She's a fighter Ruta she will be fine." Hannah rubbed my shoulder.

Eros and Arya jogged back into the clearing, their pale cheeks flushed with colour, dirt coating the bare skin of their legs. I immediately got to my feet.

"We have found another way in." Eros panted.

"Where?" Regina was pulling her belt of knives back into place.

"To the east. There is a small opening where the river runs through, once you get around the edge of it, it opens up into a natural passageway bringing you up behind the rock shelf, it's narrow to climb through, but long enough that we could all go up and over at once, they have no idea it's there." Eros grinned.

"We got right in behind them." Arya mirrored her smile.

"A natural trench." Hannah said quietly.

"Get ready!" Regina called to the waiting witches and hunters. "Take off all bulky clothing and weaponry. This is going to require stealth and precision."

"What are we going to do about Marina?" I asked.

"We kill this man that is inside her, for good this time." Regina set her mouth grimly. "If that means she has to die too, then so be it."

CHAPTER TWENTY SIX

Mia opened her eyes a crack, her mother's face a blur of colour that slowly reformed into the correct shape. Her heart thudded so slowly that she wondered if the next beat would ever come.

"Mia." Marina's voice came to her ears as though she were under water, she flicked her eyes upwards but the blackness over took her again.

Marina hissed with anger as she watched her daughters eyes close.

"I told you I didn't want to do it!" She got to her feet and began pacing back and forth as the vampires watched her berate herself. "You said it would be the best way but you were wrong!"

"My queen, who are you talking to?" One of the braver among the group dared to ask.

"Michael of course!" Marina snapped without breaking stride her eyes were wild and unfocused. The voice inside her laughed mocking her weakness.

"Shut up!" She pulled at her hair as she screamed. "Did you see what she did? The whole tree! With no more than a wave of her hands! How do you expect me to fight against that kind of power?"

"My queen, what should we do?" A small vampire asked scuttling back as she span to face them. "It looks like they are setting an attack from the trees." He added hurriedly. "The lookout said they are arranging weaponry."

Marina lowered her hands, Michael taking control of her senses fully, calmly preparing for battle.

"Let us examine this pathetic attempt." She smiled, her voice sounded lower, not quite her own, she strode up to the entrance and scanned the ground.

"You fools!" She spat. "There is nobody there apart from a few old witches laying out crossbows."

"They are hiding in the trees surely?" The vampire scout clutched his own rickety wooden shotgun to his chest, stolen from some poor man who had ventured too far off the trail and lost his life along with his gun. The clouds shifted and a beam of evening sun cut through the grey sending them scuttling back into the shadows. Marina scowled with distaste.

"Useless." She muttered stretching her mind outwards towards the heavy conifers.

"She's looking for us." Sarro paused as she splashed through the water up to her knees.

"Yeah I can feel her too." I nodded.

"Close it down Ruta do not let her in." Sarro gritted her teeth. I shut my eyes and focused hard on the image of the castle, its windows glittering in the night. We had decided that as Marina was too strong to block out it would be easier to focus on something that wouldn't give away our location and let her see that. I felt the tendrils of her consciousness carefully probing at my mind, she seemed nervous of me.

"Ruta." Sarro whispered with warning.

"It's ok." I scrunched my eyes tighter. "I know she's in there." Anger seeped through me as I felt my mother moving around my thoughts pressing trying to lift away the picture I was focusing on. I took a deep breath and changed the image to one of Mia, her face flooded with laughter as she danced through the wildflowers with Greta at her side, sunlight cascading over her ebony hair.

"You did this." I slammed every single word into my mind with as much venom as I could and felt a sense of pride as Marina practically jumped from inside my head.

"Are you ok?" Seraph asked. I nodded. "Ok let's move." She skipped along the ledge her arms outstretched for balance as the line behind followed on.

"Did you see her?" Regina asked over her shoulder, the pathway skirting the underground river was less than a foot wide and illuminated only by the faintest of light from a crack in the ceiling of the cave.

"No but I felt her I knew she was there." I wobbled as I tried to look up. "I swapped my image. I showed her Mia."

Regina didn't reply but her shoulders sagged as she caught her breath.

"Not much further." Eros whispered loud enough for us to hear. Right on cue, the voices of the vampires started to trickle towards us, the rich irony smell of blood and pungent sweat blowing through the cracks in the stone. The path turned into an alley framed on either side by soil, to our left it stretched high up curving into the roof, to the right it sloped barely two feet above our heads. Eros had been right, it was narrow with only enough space to sidle in side by side facing the compact earth.

"She is crazy I'm telling you." Regina held up a hand as a man's voice sounded directly on the other side of the wall. "At least with Vincent he knew when to give up and run."

"Yeah." Another man replied. "But what can we do now? We are stuck in here, when the girl dies she's going to be even worse."

"She doesn't look like she's got much more in her." The first man huffed. "Then we'll all be for it."

"What about that little witch eh? You ever seen anything like that? That tree damn well exploded!" The awe in his voice was clear, I lowered my eyes nervously.

"Never! Never seen nothing like it in all the years I've walked this planet. Who's this Michael she keeps talking to inside her head anyway?"

"Oh you weren't there were you, Vincent put this old vampire spirit inside her." The first vampire lowered his voice. "Bloodthirsty bastard, killed thousands in his day, looks like he's pulling the strings again." The sound of their footsteps stirred and began to move away, the conversation becoming muted. Regina waved us forwards as we all breathed a sigh of relief.

Sarro winced in pain bracing her hands against the wall, we stopped, the hunters looking up at the top of our trench nervously as the witch held back a sob of pain.

"I know you are here!" Marina shouted out triumphantly silencing the cave. "She wasn't as strong as she thought she was."

I froze as Sarro seemed to sag in what little space there was, she shook her head in silent apology.

"Come out little mice!" Marina cooed. "I saw the earth, I saw a tunnel, I know you are in here I just don't know where. Find them!" She bellowed, instantly the sound of pounding feet and clinking metal rang off the walls.

"We don't have time, move now." Regina leant forwards glancing down the line. "We have no choice we are pinned in here, let's go!" She held my gaze for a second longer than necessary a sad smile playing on her lips, then she dug her foot into the wall and powered up and over the top with a hellish scream. Beside me hunters and witches were jumping and hoisting themselves up and into the air disappearing from view, weapons clutched in their fists. I put the toe of my boot into a groove in the earth and readied myself.

"Wait!" Seraph was beside me.

"We can't wait everyone else is out there." I gawped.

"Just a few moments, they won't be expecting us if we follow after, move around this way I have a feeling up there is where your mother will be." She pointed to the left where the very edge of a shelf of rock could be seen. "We need to get to Marina."

"You planned this with Regina." I muttered. "She never had any intention of letting me go in with them did she?" Seraph shook her head.

"Not now Ruta, we can debate you being protected once this is over. We need to move." As if on cue a small black glittering ball flew overhead hitting the wall at our backs and bouncing a few feet away, I knew what it was instantly. I barely had the chance to shout run when it exploded knocking me off my feet and into Seraph.

"Ruta! Get up!" Regina appeared through the dust, her face smeared with inky blood a long curling knife in her hand. I pushed myself to my feet, looking at Seraphs back as she moved away from me snaking through the passage I stumbled behind her my ears ringing. The trench widened allowing enough space to sit down which Seraph did heavily, I looked behind me but Regina had gone.

"Are you ok?" I could hear the words inside my own head but it was obvious I was deaf to the world. Seraph beckoned me forwards placing her hands either side of my head atop my ears, a small pop and the noise hit me once more.

"Better?" She asked. I nodded.

"Are you ok?" I repeated.

"Yes." She looked behind me, Marina's head was bobbing back and forth as she fought hand to hand with one of the hunters, her fists glowing with purple light that batted the blades away effortlessly.

"How can I stop her?" I asked wincing as gunshots rang out chipping into the walls. Marina screamed with anger, raising her hands into the air and balling them into fists, a sea of metal rose up twisting and cracking as it bent in on itself before falling with a clatter back down.

"We do this the right way! No cowardice!" I trembled, that was not my mother's voice. There was a renewed flurry of swords and knives clattering against one and other.

Seraph reached for my hand and pressed a solid black vial into the palm, the stopped was out dangling limply on a silver chain.

"I have a spell that will draw him out of her. I need to be close enough for it to work." She looked at me hard. "I hate to ask it of you, but you will have to try to shield me in whatever way you can Ruta."

"How can I do that?" I spluttered.

"Your magic. It is strong, make it do what is necessary." Seraph gritted her teeth. "I know it's a long shot, it isn't stable or practiced enough but we have no other choice. She will bring this world to its knees and he is only gaining power within her." I nodded, my heart drumming in my chest.

"Once the spell is complete the soul within her will be pulled out and into this, I have already enchanted it, it knows what it is reaching for." I watched Seraph, the feeling of dread creeping into my bones, she had no idea that Michael couldn't be held in anything other than a body. The soothsayer had made it very clear, he had to be destroyed and the only way to do that was to kill the host. I lifted my head above the levelled soil and searched for my sister, finding her resting atop a long grey fur behind our mother, unmoving even amongst the chaos.

"What about Mia?" I asked.

"If she is alive still, we can heal her once Marina is controlled we have the magic to do so." Seraph spoke quickly.

"Why didn't Marina just do that then?" I frowned.

"She is powerful in some things but healing was never one of them, it takes a certain type of witch to be able to see inside a body and fix what is broken there. Ruta we really have no time, she is cutting us down." Seraph rose to her feet a tear rolling from her eye as she stared past me. I turned to look.

"No." I mumbled. Sarro was stepping carefully around Marina, circling her as my mother laughed and crooked a finger beckoning her forwards.

"This way." Seraph pulled my hand guiding me around in a clockwise circle that was bringing us ever closer to Marina and into view with each step, she saw us almost instantly.

"Ruta, darling there you are." My mother straightened up from taunting Sarro and placed her hands on her hips smiling at me. "Oh and you brought the old bat with you too." She grinned. Sarro took her moment and leapt into the air bringing down both knives in an arcing motion towards Marina's throat. I ran forwards pulling out my own short sword as my mother fell back clutching her face with one hand, blood spurted from between her fingers. Sarro charged again. A blinding purple light illuminated the cave, I shielded my eyes turning my head away.

"You cannot beat me!" Marina screamed her voice seeping into every crack, I looked back at her, a long cut stretched from her ear to chin dripping thick dark blood onto her chest. My stomach jumped into my throat and I felt the burning anger start to tingle against my skin. Sarro lay almost at my feet, her eyes wide and staring, her face smeared with earth, knife still clutched in her hand. In the centre of her chest a gaping hole, void of the brave strong heart that had nestled there only moments before. I shook from head to toe, my eyes stinging in my skull. Marina clutched the heart in her hand tightly so that it bulged between her fingers, she looked at me and smiled.

CHAPTER TWENTY SEVEN

Rage filled every single ounce of me, it shook me so hard my hands could barely keep hold of the hilt of the sword, my eyes would not tear away from the sight of Sarro's heart still and un beating clutched in my mother's hand. "Silly witch." Marina chided dropping the red mass to the floor with a thud, she wiped her hand against the leather of her trousers making it squeak sickeningly. Seraph moved to the side and slid down against the wall her head in her hands, Marina smiled at her apparent defeat but I could see the movement of her lips forming words silently. I straightened my spine and adjusted the weapon so it sat more solidly in my hand.

"Really Ruta? You really want to fight me still?" My mother cocked her head looking at me like I was a petulant child.

"Is Mia alive?" I asked. She winced slightly her face contorting oddly before becoming calm once more.

"I have no idea, but it's not much of a loss either way really she was so pathetic." The voice again sounded nothing like my mother's but it fuelled the simmering anger within me. I dropped the sword to the ground.

"Good you have seen sense." Marina sighed holding out her hands. I raised my palm and felt a rush of magic flow freely through my arm and out of the tips of my fingers, Marina's eyes widened as she was lifted off her feet and slammed into the cave wall, I walked forwards holding her there, suspended above the ground as a solid beam of red light shot from my hand coating her like a jet of water. She struggled in the flow of magic, desperately trying to lift her hands, her mouth cracked open in a scream.

"Enough!" The word bellowed all around me, I fell onto my back as the red light was extinguished, a wave of exhaustion passing over me in its wake. I forced myself to my feet. Marina was back on the ground but doubled in half and panting heavily.

"That…. Was impressive." She grunted straightening up.

"You have no idea." I hissed raising my hands once more.

"No Ruta." Regina hopped up beside me, blood splattered and muddied but not showing any signs of injury. "She is my sister, it is up to me to finish this." She pressed a hand to my shoulder and moved me back a step, Marina smiled.

"Fool. She is stronger than you!"

"That may be sister but she is un practiced and has suffered enough, you know as well as I that using much more of her magic in that amount will likely kill her or is that what you were hoping for since you don't have the strength to do it yourself?" Regina gritted her teeth. I narrowed my eyes, something was happening to my mother, the outline of her body seemed to be shimmering she frowned clutching at her side as she moved back a few steps.

"Ruta?" My mother looked up her eyes searching for me, her voice sounded frail.

"Marina." Regina moved forwards. "You have to fight him!" She grabbed her shoulders.

"She has no hope." Marina cackled throwing out her hands and sending my Aunt crashing to the floor. "Now which witch is it?" Marina turned slowly scanning the room, a debris of bodies and weapons littered the floor but the few remaining witches had assembled a few feet away. The fighting was over at least, I scanned the faces, where was Hannah?

"It's me." Regina stepped to her right, into the eye line of Marina who was glaring at the other witches, Seraph still crouched silently behind her.

"Liar, liar!" Marina squealed.

"It's me." I said stepping forwards. "I'm repeating the spell right now, over and over inside my head." Marina frowned at me, her eyes darker than before.

"Impossible." She laughed haughtily but I could see the worry coating her features.

"Not for someone with magic like mine." I continued solidly.

Regina moved forwards her knives drawn, her feet slipped on the river of blood that flowed from beneath Sarro's body, she glanced down briefly before lifting her eyes back to Marina's with a snarl.

"It seems to be a trade mark of vampires, ripping out hearts." Regina began circling, her knives clutched in her hands. "There is one thing in our favour though, every vampire that I have known to do such a disgusting cowardly thing has one thing in common."

"What is that?" Marina sneered.

"They are all dead!" Regina jumped forwards sliding to the ground and cutting at Marina's legs as she skidded past. Marina screamed jumping back, blood spurted from the back of one of her heels and her foot hung limp, she staggered trying to keep balance as Regina ran at her once more.

Another blast of purple light illuminated the walls but this time I had been ready for it, I'd sensed Marina summoning a spell and moved between my Aunt and the jet of magic, my hands raised in front of me bouncing it away. It burned into my skin and I locked my teeth together so that the scream wouldn't pass my lips, I looked into the light and saw the effort creasing my mother's face as she pressed more force into the attack.

"Ruta no!" Regina shouted behind me, I felt her hands touch my shoulders but I was unmovable. The purple began to darken, the burning intensifying, now I could feel it pressing into my flesh flaking it away from the bone. My Hands trembled and blood ran down my wrists but still I held my hands up blocking the spell.

"Now!" Seraph's voice was weak but clear, suddenly the light vanished and my mother fell flat onto her back unmoving on the stone floor, beside her a wavering apparition of a man stood looking at me in disbelief.

"How did you do that?" He demanded his voice deep and rolling with a thick accent.

"We worked together" I smiled at Seraph and threw the glass vial across to where she stood, she clutched it proudly. Michael laughed, his dark hair bobbing around his shoulders with the movement.

"You did not tell them?" He looked at me.

Behind us a loud gasp sounded, I turned to look, Mia was sitting upright, two witches beside her, the arrow now removed from her chest. I suppressed a sob as she smiled.

"So sweet." Michael said mockingly. "I cannot be contained in that, she has no way to stop me you idiots!" He laughed again.

"I won't let you ever hurt anyone else again." I looked around the room, at Sarro lifeless on the floor.

"Ruta what are you doing?" Regina asked carefully.

"I'm sorry but this is the only way." I tried not to let the fear creep into my words. "I love you all." I glanced at Mia one last time, then ran towards where Michael stood with his arms wide open, he tilted his head back and smiled as his body melted into my own.

"No Ruta!" Regina screamed starting towards me.

It is much more powerful in here. The voice echoed through my brain, I felt him pushing at my consciousness, pressing my own soul back trying to gain dominance.

"Ruta why didn't you use the vial?" Seraph came into view.

"It wouldn't work." The words felt like treacle from my mouth as I forced him to allow me to speak. "He cannot be held in anything but a human body, the soothsayer told me."

"Why didn't you tell us this?" Regina begged.

"Because If I had you would never have let me do what I need to." I groaned as he pushed at me once more.

With this power I will crush them all and you will be in here to watch

Marina stirred, her hands twitching as she tried to gather herself.

"Ruta are you still in there?" Mia had inched down from the ledge towards me, she was pale and shaking but still looked like my sister.

"Yes." I smiled.

"I'm sorry I wasn't strong like you." Mia sobbed. "If I had of fought her none of this would have happened."

"Mia, this is not your fault." I said biting back the torrent of hateful words that were tumbling from Michael's thoughts. "I don't have time." I gasped. "He is getting stronger."

"We will fix this." Regina said eagerly looking to Seraph who lowered her eyes tears spilling down her cheeks.

"It's only me that can do it now, I have to fix this Regina." I told her.

"What do you mean?" My aunt looked at me uncertainly.

"Ruta?" Mia questioned.

"Be strong Mia." I told her. "I love you all so much." I stepped back towards the ledge, moving up the ramp that led to outside.

"Where are you going?" Regina tried to follow but I waved my hand creating an invisible block that she couldn't pass through. "Ruta no!" She shouted.

"I have to do this." I could feel Michael beginning to panic as I over rode his commands. "The only way is to kill whatever he is in at the time." My feet were like lead as I hoisted them in front of one and other until the air hit my skin. I looked to the ground below. Tom was still standing sentinel and steadfast, protecting our retreat from the cave, he sniffed his long grey snout wavering in the air and then looked up at me.

I turned my eyes from his and gazed into the night, the stars speckling the inky blue with brilliant light, the trees rustling in the breeze carrying the scent of pine across the air. In the distance the glistening slates of a castle turret caught my eye, Belladon, still watching over the forest after all these years. Michael was screaming now. I stepped towards the edge looking down at the drop, it made my stomach squeeze in on itself. Regina appeared, running from the cave entrance, her dress slick with water, she looked up at me. "I love you." I pressed my mind towards her, watching as Marina ran dripping water to stand at her side.

"Ruta don't!" My mother pressed a hand to her mouth as her green eyes widened.

Yes Ruta silly girl, get back inside

Michael was fighting his way free, using the moment of indecision to claw upwards into my mind, as he became stronger I felt the anger and hate poisoning me turning me black and bitter, he would destroy the whole world in the blink of an eye and think nothing of it. I remembered the face of the little girl who had been murdered alongside her family it would be a sight mirrored all over the world if he had his way.

"I will never let that happen." I said loudly feeling him recoil. "I'm sorry." I looked at the gathered faces below, Seraph was holding onto Mia tightly as she hid her head against the older woman's shoulder. "But I have to do this. Don't forget what we are here for, we are the ones who protect the innocent and destroy evil, that is what we do. What we were born for, no matter what the cost." I drew in a long deep breathe feeling my lungs expand, noticing the way they moved against my chest, my legs trembled.

"Ruta." The voice was gentle but so close it made me jump.

"Hannah?" I moved back a step to where the woman was slumped against the wall, blood spilling from her mouth, she clutched at a large gaping hole in her side.

"Come here." She beckoned me closer, I knelt at her side allowing her to reach up pressing her head to mine holding the back of my neck with her hand. Something tugged at my navel, turning me inside out as the world span around me, I heard Michael scream then everything fell quiet. Hannah held the black glass vial in her hand her thumb over the opening.

I patted myself down, my fingers sticking to a long thin cut just above my hip bone.

"Did you just put him in there?" I gasped.

"Yes but it won't hold him for long." Hannah's voice seemed to gurgle.

"He has to be destroyed Hannah." I began but she was nodding.

"I'm dying Ruta I can't be saved, the wound is too bad. Seraph told me what to do to draw him out, the magic in this is so strong that contact with any open wound is enough to pull him in." She drew in a quaking breathe and tapped the black glass. "Look after Regina for me and tell her that I do love her." She moved her thumb and tipped the vial to her lips forming a seal around the bottle.

I sat silently staring at her as her eyes widened and became blackened at the edges.

"What have you done?" Hannah's mouth moved but it was almost entirely Michael's voice. "This body is weak!"

"You will know death in it most absolute form." I told him as Hannah pressed herself to her feet.

"He is trying to gain power over me Ruta I don't have much time before I can't control him." Hannah clutched at my hand moving towards the edge. "I guess this is it."

"You can't do this." I clutched her arm as she moved to step off into the air.

"You know I have to Ruta." She smiled softly. "I am dying anyway, why not let it achieve something hey?" I tried to find an argument to persuade her that she was wrong, but knew deep down there was none.

"Hannah?" Regina shouted as she looked up at us. Hannah drew in a sharp breath, her eye's meeting my Aunt's.

"I love you." The words were a whisper, then she was gone.

CHAPTER TWENTY EIGHT

I stared down at the ground, Hannah lay still, her body bent at awkward angles.

"Regina." Seraph tried to catch my aunt's hand as she moved closer but she shrugged her off and stepped around the pool of blood that was spreading through the dirt. I tried to make myself look away but found I couldn't, I was rooted in disbelief. Regina knelt at Hannah's side, brushing the stray strand of blonde hair back from her face and softly closing the lids of her eyes, she looked up at me tears rolling down her face.

"Why didn't you stop her?" She shouted, her voice snapping off the rock face.

"I couldn't.... she was dying.... She said she couldn't be healed." I stammered.

"Regina, it's true. The wound she had in her side was too deep to be fixed, she had already lost so much blood that her body was shutting down. She made a very brave decision, one that has saved a lot of people from a lot of pain and loss." Seraph rested a hand on Regina's shoulder as the younger witch sagged in sorrow.

"What about me? It hasn't saved me from pain." She broke into tears her shoulders heaving.

A few feet above Hannah's body a fine black dust had begun to swirl, I tilted my head squinting my eyes to try to see more clearly.

"Move!" Seraph grabbed Regina pulling her to her feet and scampering back a few strides. The dust was thickening, moulding into the shape of a human body, a man, broad and tall. Marina whimpered.

"Michael." I felt my lip curl with anger as he appeared more solidly the tiny black particles fusing together.

"Oh dear." He flicked his eyes at Hannah's body. "What a waste!" His voice had a watery rippling tone to it. "Did you really think that would kill me?" He crooked his eyebrow and tutted theatrically. "I cannot be killed! The spell that was placed on me meant that I was separated entirely from my body, no body equals nothing to destroy!" He grinned.

"Come, live inside me, see how well you get on." Regina was straining as Seraph held her tightly by her arms.

"No you are quite right, I don't think that combination would go so well." He turned his head to where Mia was standing, wide eyed and quivering next to our mother. "We have established that you will if necessary, kill that one." He pointed a thumb at Marina who winced and scuttled backwards. "But I don't think you could bring yourself to kill her." He pointed at Mia who almost fell to the floor her knees where knocking together so badly. I felt the rage building inside me, the magic ebbing into my hands, even my eyes seemed to burn in their sockets.

"Hey Michael." I called, every head turned towards me as I stepped off the edge of the cliff. A gasp ran through the gathered witches and Seraph opened her mouth to scream, halting as I floated gently down towards the ground, the stream of light from my palms burrowing into the soil slowing my descent like a jet pack. Even Michael looked slightly worried. Close up the particles holding his form together were as I suspected, vibrating at high speed bumping each other in an effort to stay in the correct shape.

"Impressive little witch." He smiled turning to face me.

"Oh you have no idea." I grinned back.

"You can't stop what will happen in this world." Michael was nervous at my apparent lack of fear. "If it was not me it would be another Baron, another Vincent! Our kind is tired of hiding in the shadows, we will rise up and we have the power to do so." His voice had risen as though addressing a crowd of followers. "With her at our helm" He pointed to where Marina stood "There will always be the possibility of a new race, her nature will overcome her desire to be good and you can't kill me! I will always be present in one way or another." He smiled broadly.

"There is one flaw in your theory Michael." I stepped forwards. "You see throughout the whole of time there has been people like you, people who want to watch the world burn and crumble just because they are so angry and bitter. Broken men and women who think that by commanding others to commit hideous crimes against innocent people it somehow makes them special, it doesn't, it makes you a monster." I told him my voice calm and quiet. "I am happy to be that monster, I will be remembered!" He boomed, the particles shaking faster.

"Yes, maybe." I nodded. "A lot of bad people are remembered, it's a good thing that they are." He frowned at me. "Because every single one of them ended up defeated, their acts of hate and war did nothing but join good people together, united in grief and struggle and those people are more powerful than any magic or strength you believe you have." I smiled. "You will be gone soon and yes another may decide to act in the same silly way." I rolled my eyes and shrugged with a sigh. "Then we will have to kill them too."

"I'm not dead little girl. You couldn't kill me, you tried and failed!" He laughed tilting his head back.

"No you're right I can't kill you, but I can contain you." I lifted my hands quickly, praying that the words thundering through my mind would translate into magic. There was a split second where nothing happened and Michaels face relaxed slightly as though he were about to laugh, then blinding blue light shot from my hands encasing every single speck of dust. A rumbling echoed off the walls of the mountainside, spreading through the treetops sending birds cawing and flapping from their nests, I scrunched my eyes tight as I felt the flow of magic subsiding and exhaustion sweeping over me, as quickly as it had come it vanished and I fell back against the ground the world melting into darkness.

"Ruta." Mia nudged my arm gently. "I saw her eyes open." She spoke quickly.
"Yep, I did too." I recognised Greta's voice.
"Ok girls give her a little bit of space." Anita said quietly, something soft and cool was placed over my eyes darkening the lids. I moved my lips, my throat felt dry and sore.
"See her mouth just opened." Mia said excitedly.
"Go get your Aunt." Anita said and I heard a scuffling of feet.
"Where am I?" I croaked.
"You are at the cavern Ruta. You are safe." Anita soothed. "Here drink this." She placed her hand behind my head and tilted it upwards, I felt a cup at my lips and sipped, the sweet thick nectar running over my tongue and down my scratchy throat easing the pain.

"Thank you." My voice sounded better. "What is over my eyes?" I asked raising a hand.

"It's clay from the river bed." Anita moved my hand away softly. "Your sight will be a little blurry for a while but your eyes are healing well, this helps heal the burns." She lifted the clay pack from my face and I cracked the lids open. Everything looked blurry.

"Why can't I see properly Anita?" I panicked pushing myself into a sitting position.

"Stay calm Ruta, it will return to normal." I turned my head, I could make out where Anita stood, the colours of her skin and hair the only things visible.

"Ruta you are awake." I span to look at where the doorway must have been and squinted at the dark hair tumbled around the white narrow shape of a face.

"Regina?" I questioned.

"Yes and your mother is here and Mia and Seraph." She moved towards me and I saw more shapes entering the room.

"Seraph now that she is awake can you do anything?" Regina asked grabbing my hand.

"I can try." Seraph moved towards me, I could smell the smoke on her hands as she reached up and placed the palms against my face. My brow creased as a chill coated my eyes, I could feel it spreading to the back of my skull like water being poured in.

"Any better?" Seraph asked moving her hands. The cold subsided and I opened my eyes.

"Yes I can actually see you now." I smiled as everyone came into focus. "If I turn my head it still blurs a little."

"It's ok, time will heal the rest." Seraph patted my leg and moved away.

"When you said that it took special magic to heal people you never said that you had that magic?" I said watching as the older witch turned to smile.

"I don't really, not on a deep level, I can't mend broken bones or fix a pierced heart." She looked at Mia who grinned. "But I can do small things."

"What happened?" I asked looking at Regina.

"There will be time to talk about that, you need to rest, all is ok." She smiled.

"No I need to know what happened Regina, please." I took her hand and squeezed it gently.

"Ok." She held up a hand as Marina began to protest, my mother fell back glancing at me sheepishly. "Well, we are still not sure how you did it, but you turned Michael to stone." I gawped at her. "Whatever came from you was so powerful, it fused all the particles of what used to be his body and turned them to stone, it's encased him entirely, we were going to smash it up and scatter the pieces but we're not sure whether breaking it would mean that it would all come flying free and anyway, it's like granite I'm not sure we could crack it if we tried." Regina smiled. "He will never be able to control anyone again Ruta, thanks to you."

"It's a shame I didn't know I could do it sooner." I sagged against the bed of moss. "Maybe then Sarro and Hannah would still be here." At the mention of Sarro's name my mother gave a sob and darted from the room.

"Is she ok?" I asked watching Mia quickly follow down the tunnel.

"They will be." Seraph sighed. "I will go and make sure they have everything they need to take with them." She added to Regina.

"What does she mean, take with them?" I asked.

"Later. You need to rest." Anita looked at my aunt pointedly.

"It's not your fault, none of it, remember that." Regina squeezed my hand tighter and turned to leave.

"Where are they?" I asked quietly. "I need to see them."

Regina eyed me carefully, large round tears coating the surface of the lavender orbs.

"Regina she really needs to rest." Anita pleaded.

"I can't rest until I have seen them." I said softly. Regina nodded showing she understood.

"Come, I will take you to them."

CHAPTER TWENTY NINE

Knowing that Hannah and Sarro were gone was one thing, standing in front of their graves was something else entirely.

"I never even knew this part of the cavern existed." I muttered looking around.

"Yes well I suppose it's one of those places that you don't really want to come to unless you have to." Seraph said sadly.

"It's beautiful though." A fine trickle of water ran down the inside of the stone wall, pooling into a sunken rockery before gently creeping out through a gap in the wall. Thick green moss coated the floor and a beam of sunlight shone through from the sky above, shooting between the overlapping slabs of stone that formed the ceiling. Small wildflowers grew in abundance at the water's edge and dark green ivy climbed up the walls, the two headstones sat nestled amongst them. I swallowed hard seeing the names carved with swirling letters into stone.

"It doesn't seem real." I shook my head.

"But unfortunately it is." Regina placed her hand atop the slab that bore Hannah's name and looked down pain creasing her face.

"She said she loved you." I spoke quietly, Regina looked at me her eyes ringed with red from her tears. "That was the last thing she said." Regina bit her bottom lip and nodded dropping her head to her chest.

"Come." Seraph gently turned my shoulder and led me back through the tunnel towards the main hall. "She needed to hear that Ruta, but it will be hard to take." She added patting my shoulder. "She should be alone to deal with it." We walked slowly into the open space, I looked around noticing the sudden hush as I appeared. The witches stopped what they were doing and turned to look at me. I froze, did they blame me for Hannah's death? Where they afraid of me after seeing the magic I'd used? I jumped as a cheer rang out.

"Ruta! Princess of the witches!" Somebody yelled from the back as the clapping and cheering loudened. I was engulfed by women patting my back and planting kisses on my cheeks, shaking my hands and shoulders, squeezing my face in their hands.

"Enough now sisters." Seraph smiled. "Back to your tasks let the girl be." They dispersed and I looked at my great aunt with confusion.

"What you did was very powerful magic Ruta, you rid an evil from this world that has undoubtedly saved hundreds of thousands of people from pain and suffering. You are a hero to them." She explained.

"I'm not a hero." I lowered my eyes. "Hannah was the hero if she hadn't of allowed Michael into her body and then... did what she did, he would never have been free for me to trap him."

"That is true and not at all forgotten, they will remember her always and all who have left us too soon along with her." Seraph assured me.

"Where is he?" I asked.

"Michael? He was taken to the castle to be held securely in the dungeons." Her face flushed red and she looked away.

"What?" I questioned.

"Ruta don't get angry before you understand." Seraph faced me, I remained silent but looked at her expectantly. "Your mother and Mia were taken there too."

"What do you mean taken there? Against their will?" I could feel the anger rising I took a breath and pushed it down.

"Well, no not against their will. They agreed to go, but they are to be held there." Seraph said carefully.

"What like prisoners?" I baulked.

"No, not exactly. They will be contained but well cared for." I began to protest but Regina strode in to view silencing me.

"What can we do Ruta? They are vampire in part, we cannot let them wander freely around the country, especially not your mother we have no idea if she can control any impulses she might have, we had no time to establish how it affected her being locked in Vincent's possession for all those years." She stood in front of me hands on hips. "They will be well cared for. They have an entire cabin to themselves with access to the woods in part, we ringed the area with a high silver chain link fence so that they can go outside and walk around freely. They both agreed to enter the area Ruta."

"The prison, call it what it is Regina." I spat.

"It isn't a prison if they entered it out of choice Ruta!" She hissed back. "It is hard for us too, knowing they will be in there but there is nothing we can do until we are sure it is safe for them to be completely free."

I knew she was right. "Can we go to the castle?" I asked.

"Yes of course, give yourself a few days to build up some strength and we will leave as soon as you wish." Seraph smoothed a hand over my hair before moving away.

"I'm sorry." I muttered to my Aunt. "It's just so hard to take, all this to free my mother and now she is going to be locked up again and Mia with her." I stubbed my toe into the earth.

"I know." Regina reached out and pulled me into a hug. "It's not fair but neither is life."

"We will be able to help them wont we?" I pressed my face to her shoulder.

"I hope so Ruta, I really hope so."

Conker snorted and pranced as he watched me coming closer.

"Did you miss me?" I laughed as he butted his head into my chest lifting me off my feet with a nicker. He swung his nose around towards the saddle grabbing the stirrup in his teeth and holding it outwards for me.

"Ok I get it!" I hopped up onto his back and felt him bouncing with energy.

"Regina are you ready because I think my friend here may be about to explode!" I laughed again as he lifted his front feet in tiny circles trying his hardest not to dash forwards.

"Yes let's go." Regina smiled and moved into the forest leading us towards the trail. Seraph and Matisse strode ahead, the obligatory stream of smoke blowing behind them. Conker jogged through the trees, his head bouncing up and down as he skipped over branches and rabbit holes.

It felt strange not checking the trees for any sign of lurking vampires, almost all of them had been killed during the fighting. Tom loped along at my side his paws padding through the shrubs, his coat shone dappled with the light peeking through the canopy of leaves.

"Mind this fool doesn't step on your tail." I said jokingly as Conker sidestepped an upturned log snorting. Tom flicked his yellow eyes to us and gave a toothy grin breaking into a trot that took him weaving between tree trunks and out of sight.

"See you scared him away now." I laughed. We moved along the trail, I watched Seraph and Regina talking to one and other, each had a hand resting on their horses neck the other clutching the rope reins, ebony hair fanning around their shoulders, the family resemblance was suddenly very clear.

"Hi!" Tom was leaning against the trunk of a tree his voice made me jump, Conker squealed and flicked his heels into the air before gathering himself and acting as though nothing had happened. Tom smiled and fell into step walking beside us.

"I could have landed on my head then." I told him righting myself in the saddle.

"Well you wouldn't have hurt anything then would you?" Tom smiled as I slapped at his head. We moved along the path in silence for a few minutes, I could see him chewing his bottom lip, his cheeks reddening nervously. He reached up and halted Conker, holding onto the rein and looking at me earnestly.

"I'm not sorry for kissing you." He blurted out. "I know I said I was sorry, but I'm not." His face flushed an even deeper shade of crimson but he held his head high.

"Ok." I smiled not knowing what to say. "That's good to know I guess."

"I like you Ruta, I can't help it." He lowered his eyes for a second. "I know I shouldn't but I do." I looked at him, realising that my stomach was flipping, noticing for the first time the sharp line of his jaw, the smooth cheekbones that angled up to his kind oval eyes.

"Do you like me?" He mumbled flicking his eyes from mine back to the ground.

"I.... um... yes." I fumbled over my words blushing.

"Maybe we could spend some time together, doing stuff." He smiled broadly. "Watch a movie or something." He shrugged.

"Yeah that sounds good." I smiled back.

"Tom if you had a tail right now it would be wagging so hard you would be propelled off the ground." I looked to my right where the path had curved widely without me noticing, Regina and Seraph both sat on their horses with smiles playing on their lips. Seraph flicked the growing ash from her cigarette and arched an eyebrow expectantly.

"I should go ahead." Tom muttered letting go of the piece of rope and disappearing into the trees once more, a second later a wolf skipped back past us his ears lowered as Regina eyed him carefully. He looked up at Seraph and his broad bushy tail flew from side to side, she suppressed her grin as Regina huffed loudly. Tom trotted away quickly down the path.

"What the hell was that?" Regina leant forwards.

"What?" I asked quickly moving Conker alongside Seraph.

"He kissed you? When?" Regina demanded kicking Aura on, the mare grunted and swished her tail in annoyance.

"I'm not answering your questions Regina." I blushed.

"Quite right to!" Seraph chuckled.

"You will answer me young lady." Regina scolded.

"I feel like a gallop, do you?" Seraph smiled at me meaningfully.

"Yes I think that's a great idea." I laughed and gave Conker a pat. "Let's go boy!" I shouted as we sprang forwards.

"I can still ask questions at speed you know!" Regina barked from behind us. The wind whipped my hair from my face, taking my breath away, I tucked my chin in lowering myself against the flame red neck feeling the earth spinning away beneath us. My heart hammered in my ears and for the first time in a long while, I felt alive.

CHAPTER THIRTY

Mia swung her feet over the edge of the wall, banging them so that the heels of her shoes made a clipping noise against the stone. I threw another pebble into the river.

"It's not so bad you know." She sipped from a travel mug that Henry had given her. "You can't even see it through this." She tapped her finger against the green metal side.

"Yes, but you are still sitting next to me slurping a pint of deer blood!" I turned away crinkling my nose.

"At least it's not all the time." Mia shut the lid and shoved the mug into her backpack.

"That's true." I nodded watching Greta and Anita splashing in the shallow water hopping over pebbles.

"Do you think mother will ever be able to come back out into the real world?" Mia asked quietly. I sighed and looked across the meadow. Several weeks had passed since we had arrived back at the castle, Mia had taken to the diet of deer blood once a day mixed with regular human food and was showing no signs of any kind of vampire cravings. My mother on the other hand was still struggling to curb her instincts.

"I don't know Mia." I admitted. "I mean it could be worse, at least she's here with us, she sees us every day she has her own home, garden space." I patted my hand against the rough wall. Marina was still contained in one of the billets, Regina had had it gutted and made into a real home, open plan living room with log fire, an upstairs bedroom and bathroom she even had the fence line extended to include part of the river. But the diet of deer blood hadn't been enough, she would fly into rages, launching at the fence when the scent of human blood was close and it only seemed to be worsening. Dr Vause had taken to asking the students to donate blood and was using this to suppress my mother's outbursts, so far it was working but nothing was certain.

"Do you think she could live in there forever and be happy?" Mia looked at me with hope.

"She says she could." I shrugged. We fell into silence once more.

"Hey what are you two up to?" Regina moved through the long grass towards us.

"Just chatting." I smiled.

"Come down into the river." She signalled us towards her.

"I'm ok." I said as Mia hopped down.

"Oh come on Ruta." She tugged my hand.

"No honestly you go, I need to be somewhere." I told her swinging my legs around and moving towards the forest.

"See you later?" Mia asked.

"See you later." I shouted over my shoulder as I picked my way through the nettles before reaching a well worn path between the trees, I headed towards the billets.

"Hi." My mother lifted her head as I pushed through the bushes and moved alongside the fence.

"Ruta." She smiled.

"How are you?" I asked sitting on the ground opposite her, we had stopped going in after she had thrown a medical student across the enclosure in one of her rages.

"I'm good." She nodded.

"I feel as though I'm visiting you in jail." I told her as I tapped the silver linked fencing.

"To be honest after the things I've done, it should probably be a real jail. This is just home, space limited, but home." She looked down at her feet.

"But none of it was your fault." I repeated a sentence we had all been saying to her.

"I know, but still, it happened." Her face darkened.

"Do you think you could be happy in there?" I asked looking around. "I mean if it was permanent."

"I am happy Ruta." She smiled and her face genuinely relaxed for the first time. "I have everything I need and want, I get to see my beautiful girls every single day. I feel safe in here."

I nodded I understood how she felt. I looked up at the turreted walls of the castle, its windows shining in the light, the newly rebuilt tower stood out with clean clear stone against the ivy covered older granite. Students were milling over the lawns in the sunlight, laughing and shouting to one and other.

"It's a fortress this place isn't it." I squinted up at the roof the petrol blue tiles sloping up to the sky.

"Yes. As long as it's here there will always be hope." Marina agreed, we turned our heads as Dr Vause came stepping across the grass towards us.

"I have some news." He puffed clutching his side. "When we took blood from the students Ruta and Mia donated as well as Regina and Seraph." He straightened up clutching a piece of paper in his hand. "Well I had an idea, if we gave you only their blood Marina, for a few days, I wondered if it would jump start your own DNA forcing it to react."

"And?" My mother shot to her feet.

"It's working." He patted the paper. "Your adrenaline levels have returned to almost normal, your human cells are regenerating. It won't work completely because we can't eradicate your whole blood type but we should be able to get it down to the same level as Mia's." I gawped at the doctor as he looked from face to face. "Within three days you have had no outbursts, no spikes in adrenaline, no rushes of uncontrollable anger and this morning the blood we gave you was from a deer not a human. It sustained you." He shook the paper again.

"I can't believe it." I whispered.

"It's incredible." He agreed nodding his head.

"This means that I will be able to hug my children again." Marina broke into a sob pressing her fingers to the links of the fence, I winced as they sizzled against the silver.

"I keep forgetting about that." Marina laughed and shook her hand in the air.

"After all these years and all the things we have been through, you will really be free!" I cried.

"What's going on?" Regina called from behind us, Mia and Greta were skipping ahead, both soaking wet with Seraph dawdling behind, her arm clutched in the nook of Henry's elbow.

"Doctor I will let you explain." I waved my hands towards them turning to my mother as the chorus of voices chattered excitedly behind us.

"Do you feel any different?" I asked.

"I felt calmer, sleepy almost." Marina's eyes shone brightly although the dark black ring still scarred the colour, a reminder of her suffering.

"Open the gateway." Regina barked pulling at the latch, shoving the hunter who was stationed on guard.

"Yes, do it." Henry urged as the man looked at him for confirmation.

"Regina don't maybe it's not safe yet." Marina held her hands up backing away.

"You have always been my sister." Regina flung the gate wide and strode into the open space. "I have known you your entire life, your heart is good." She threw her arms around my mother's neck lifting her feet off the floor, the pair of them toppled to the ground laughing.

"Come on!" I nudged Mia and ran through holding her hand tightly, we jumped into the mass of tangled arms and legs.

"My girls." Marina sobbed pulling each of us close in her arms. Regina stood up backing away watching us with a huge smile, tears rolling down her face.

"I can't believe we have another chance." She sobbed.

"There will always be hope of a happy ending." Henry pulled Regina to him clutching her against his chest, Seraph wiped a stray tear away quickly. "While this castle is here and the people in it remain true and brave, there will always be good to fight the evil and therefore there will always be light at the end of all dark tunnels. As long as there is Belladon anyone who falls will always have a friend to reach down and stretch out a hand to help pull them back to their feet." Regina smiled.

"Yes and anyone who carries darkness in their heart, any being who wishes to cause pain and suffering, should be afraid because there is no fight we cannot win." Seraph added her voice warbling despite her best effort to control it.

"Well said." Henry looked at her his eyes soft and full of pride. Regina noticed the moment and edged away.

"Do you think Anise would be proud of us?" Seraph asked looking up at him.

"Oh yes, I think she would be cracking open a vintage bottle of whiskey and a crate of cigars. It would be time for a party that is for sure." He laughed as Regina joined us with a battle cry and giant leap piling atop as we pushed each other. "She would be proud of her girls." He wiped away a stray tear.

"Your girls." Seraph corrected quietly. Henry stared at her blankly his face frozen. "They are your girls Henry. Both Regina and Marina, how could they be anybody else's?" She frowned at him.

"She never told me." Henry spluttered.

"She didn't have to." Seraph's voice was lightly scolding. "You knew Henry, there was nobody else she ever loved." He covered his mouth his hand smoothing down the sides of his white moustache.

"Do they know?" His voice was croaky.

"No." Seraph shook her head. "But there is all the time in the world to tell them now." She smiled.

"How strange, they have saved this castle without ever knowing that it really is their family home." He shook his head with disbelief.

"Look at them Henry, this has always been their home." Seraph pointed to where we were jostling each other, Mia leapt up joined by Greta and Tom in his wolf form and raced out of the pen towards the river bank leaping into the water with a splash, Regina whooped and chased after them. Marina stopped at the line of the gate and eyed the open ground nervously.

"Come on!" Regina shouted looking over her shoulder. "It's ok come on!" She called, Marina hesitated then burst into a sprint laughing as she overtook Regina who, competitive as ever dug in her heels and tried to catch up. I watched them running through the grass, the long stems sweeping across their bare legs, ebony hair glinting in the sunlight, the horses grazing in the meadow lifted their heads and looked on with interest. I closed my eyes breathing in deeply, the smell of the pine trees carrying on the breeze. It really was good to be home.

In the cellar of the castle, a mouse scuttled through the dust sniffing at the thick wooden bars of a tall crate. Silver chains wrapped around its sides anchoring into large iron rings that were set into the walls. The mouse lifted its face, long whiskers twitching back and forth listening for any sound amongst the piles of boxes. It lifted its paws to the thick links of the chain and scuttled up quickly, poking its head between the wooden slats to eye the stone figure of a man. He sat silently examining the statue, pink nose wavering in the air. The stone was solid and still, the mouse happy with this moved back down the side and into the shadows running along the edge of the wall and back into his hole out of sight. The statue blinked.

With unending thanks to the best person in the whole
World, my mum. Without you nothing would have been
Possible. To my sister who is my real life hero,
Imogen and Liam, Julie and the boys (both big and little)
And all my family and friends who have supported me
Through all of my writing! Huge thanks to you all! And
As J.K.Rowling said… no story lives unless someone wants
To listen…. So thank you for listening!

xxxx

Printed in Great Britain
by Amazon